CRAIG'S LIST CHRONICLES

byte-size
TALES

For more information or to book an event, please contact Barbonibooks@gmail.com

Cover Design & Illustration by Tracey Berglund
Cover Photograph by Teo González
Edits by Robert Rodi
Author Photograph by Tal Shaptnzer
Book Art Production by Kim Masson

Images sources: Wikipedia Creative Commons, Kim Masson, Philip Bump/Flicker, StaffordGreenO/Pixabay

Craig's List Chronicles / by Kim Masson.—1st ed
p.cm.
Library of Congress Control Number: 2016935872

ISBN 978-0-9974059-1-0

Printed in United States of America
10 9 8 7 6 5 4 3 2 1

For Teo

Dear Craig,

You don't know me yet, but give me enough time and we'll be the best of friends. It's okay if you don't believe me. One of these days you will discover I'm like Spanish moss—soft and inviting, tough to get rid of, and growing on everything. You see, my name is Kelly B., a concrete-jungle native and your chosen guide to my fair city, NYC. Consider me your genie in a bottle, ready to dispense insight and dispel urban fallacies. In New York, truth is relative, and only a good guide can be trusted to help sort through such things. Do yourself a favor: don't believe everything you see on TV.

But before we get into all the do's and don'ts, would it be too bold if I gave you a Big Apple embrace? Please don't mind the sweet hint of cinnamon, it's only my perfume. I find the scent cuts through the acrid misconceptions people usually make about my kind before they arrive here. It's better to find out early on that not all us are trash-talking boneheads who drive like animals and wear scowls like badges of honor. In fact, we're quite the opposite. For instance, catch us after we've snagged a taxi in the pouring rain and you'd swear we're the most grateful people on Earth.

Not everything I say is guaranteed, of course. The moment you try to replace a driver's license, or go to the post office with that pink package slip, all bets are off, because—feel free to insert a "fuggedaboutit" here—you have just entered into a bureaucratic nightmare that rivals the noble Romans'.

No need to worry, though; there are plenty of avenues to avoid such vulgarities. After all, this is the city of hopes and dreams, and boy do we have plenty of dreamers. See the Empire State Building? Yeah, that was somebody's dream. That wet-windowed noodle shop on the corner of Canal Street? Yup, you guessed it, another guy's dream. Everywhere you look a person is dreaming. Shit, I'm still dreaming for the sidewalks to turn into gold and to kiss Prince Charming. I know there are no such things, but that can't stop a girl from fantasizing.

Enough about me, let's move on to you. I realize we've never met before, so don't chalk me up as some kind of stalker, but I must say you certainly know how to create a buzz. There's a lot of gossip flying around and I'm hoping you can put some of these things to rest. Is it really true you're from San Francisco? People have been stitching up all sorts of exotic stories, like you're a Jersey Shore original or that you grew up in Boca Raton, of all places. Either way, keep those last two buried and stick with San Fran; take it from me, it has built-in cachet. Flash that card here and you'll get into all the right places. I don't know if it's those hills or that healthy Cali lifestyle, but I'm betting you won't find a shortage of people who are into you solely based on their perceptions of your geographic origin. Hey, the French got their sexy accent and the Eiffel Tower; you've got mysterious fog and organic living. How's that for curb appeal?

Speaking of which, there are also rumors floating around that you've got calves like baseball bats and are always one step away from the next hot event. Hello Mr. Perfect! With stats like the ones you're racking up, you'd best put an extra lock on your door—all the guys and gals will be lining up outside like it's the next Barney's sample sale. See Craig, words fly almost as fast as our Silver Bullet trains, and I wasn't exaggerating when I said *everyone* is talking about you coming to town. You're like Santa minus the red suit and big belly. I heard you've got all kind of goodies in your bag: shoes, furniture, books, jobs, even love. Where do you find the time to juggle so many items? I guess that's where those lists come in. I wonder if I tried making more lists whether I'd become as popular, or at the very least as organized, as you. I can barely tie my shoelaces and I still scribble notes on my hand. It's no wonder I'm still single.

Got a list for poor lonely souls looking for love into too many dive bars and dusty library corners? I'm dead serious. I've got more cobwebs down there than I care to admit. Pickings are slim these days and I could really use some outside help. My last date's idea of dinner was a bottomless bucket of onion rings, which he ate with a personalized spork. No joke. There have got to be better options out there.

So please, if you know any guys interested in meeting a cool single gal in her twenties who can't whistle, but can do a pirouette and kick a mean roundhouse at the same time, let me know. My bragging rights include (in no particular order): being a one-time hand model, getting kissed by macho-man Randy Savage in a Florida airport, and once needing rescuing from a runaway camel in the middle of the Moroccan desert.

And oh, did I mention I'm a natural blonde who can count beyond ten without using my fingers?

Here's the thing, if I don't find a male to talk about soon, my mother has plans to set me up with her work buddy Betsy—the woman's beard is thicker than my Dad's and she's got the biggest Kermit the Frog collection in the lower 48 states. That's right, since I can't get a guy in my clutches, my mom is pimping me out as a lesbian. See what I'm dealing with? All I have to say is thank God you and those coveted lists are coming to town! Who knows, I'm in the market for a couch, maybe I'll find love while I'm at it. Funnier things have happened, right? I'm sure you're the man who knows.

So, look...I know you are a busy guy running around doing deals all day and I don't want to take up any more of your time. If you've got any questions, just give a shout. I'm available 24/7. Like my city, we genies aren't prone to sleeping. And hey, once you've settled in, if you can conjure me up a list of all those cool guys you know, I'd totally appreciate it. As you've heard, looking for love in the Big Apple has given me nothing but pits.

Let's chat soon!
Your new friend,

Kelly

P.S.: If any of them look like Keanu Reeves, don't be shy, just send them my way!

posted: 2000-06-13 3:33pm EDT

Man seeks woman to explore NYC and enjoy some snuggling

Hello, I am a 26 yr. old man seeking a smart sexy woman to join me on an adventure. I am a recent business school grad from Boston who just moved to New York City. I'm interested in meeting a special someone who can help show me around my new town.

I'd like to meet someone who shares my interests, but she must be independent and have ideas of her own to bring to the table. I love traveling, reading good books, and hiking outdoors. I also enjoy going to the movies and checking out art museums. If you like good food, then you will be in good hands. I know my way around the kitchen, and if we hit it off I promise to cook you plenty of nice meals. I speak two languages and have been known to make a mean apple martini.

I am athletic, 6'2", with black hair and green eyes. Some people say I look like Keanu Reeves. Drop me a line if you like what you read. I'd love to hear from you.

- Location: New York
- It's NOT okay to solicit this person with services or other unrelated interests

To: twereta19876342@pers.cl.org
Date: June 14th, 2000 11:02 a.m.

Subject: Man seeks woman to explore NYC and enjoy some snuggling

Dear man seeks woman,

A friend forwarded your posting, believing we'd make a good match. It seems like we share a lot of the same interests. I'm also a lover of books, but my passion is writing. I lived in Amherst, Massachusetts for 4 years while attending college. NYC is my hometown, so if you've got any questions, feel free to ask. I'm an experienced traveler; my last trip was to Seville, Spain. It's a beautiful city which I highly recommend if you've never been.

At the moment, I'm working for a magazine publishing company as a Research Analyst. I work with a lot of numbers and help write up sales specs for advertisers. It is super boring work. A few years ago I taught a cooking class through the Learning Annex. That was a lot of fun. I would love to switch jobs to something more creative.

I know they still haven't figured out a way to send pictures through the site—I'm guessing we're still in beta mode—so I'll try my best to describe my looks. I am 5'7", have strawberry blonde hair and weigh about 120 lbs. I was trained in classical ballet, and even though I haven't done it since high school, my body has remained pretty toned. Like you, I also have green eyes.

If you're interested in learning more, shoot me an email at the address above. If not, no hard feelings. I wish you good luck in the hunt!

All the best,
Kelly

From: Marcus Khan <marcusk@aol.com>
To: Kelly B <kellyb@hotmail.com>
Date: June 14th, 2000 1:15 p.m.

Re: Man seeks woman to explore NYC and enjoy some snuggling

Hi Kelly,

I just finished reading your letter and I must say I am extremely intrigued. A writer, former ballerina, *and* knowledgeable local who can cook? That's quite a potent combination! Also, I must admit I've got a thing for strawberry blondes. This friend of yours seems to have excellent taste. I haven't been to Spain yet, but it's definitely on my list of places to see. I recently got back from an amazing trip to Nepal where I hiked up Mount Everest. It was the thrill of my life. Would you be interested in grabbing some drinks and exchanging travel stories? Sorry if I'm being too forward, I'm new to the whole Internet dating thing.

Cheers,
Marcus

From: Kelly B
To: Marcus Khan <marcusk@aol.com>
Date: June 14th, 2000 4:57 p.m.

Re: Man seeks woman to explore NYC and enjoy some snuggling

No worries, you're not being too forward. I'd love to meet up and exchange some travel stories. God knows I've got plenty of wacky tales to share! Nepal must have been an incredible trip. I can't wait to hear all about it. Instead of drinks, would you be interested in checking out some art? There are a lot of great exhibits going on and I think it could be fun. Believe it or not, I've never been on an Internet date either. I'd be happy to embark on a maiden voyage with you. Who knows, if things go well I might even throw in a snuggle or two :)

-Kelly

From: Marcus Khan
To: Kelly B <kellyb@hotmail.com>
Date: June 15th, 2000 3:23 p.m.

Re: Man seeks woman to explore NYC and enjoy some snuggling

How could any man say no to such an offer? A day viewing art is great idea. I wish I was cool enough to come up with it first. I'm free to link up on Saturday. Got any place in mind? I'm open to anything.

From: Kelly B
To: Marcus Khan <marcusk@aol.com>
Date: June 15th, 2000 8:59 p.m.

Re: Man seeks woman to explore NYC and enjoy some snuggling

Feel like checking out some mummies at the Met? Saturday works for me, too. How about we meet at the top of the steps around noon? I'll wear my cute camo bag so you won't miss me.

From: Marcus Khan
To: Kelly B <kellyb@hotmail.com>
Date: June 15th, 2000 10:01 p.m.

Re: Man seeks woman to explore NYC and enjoy some snuggling

Unfortunately, I don't have a cute camo bag so I hope you won't mind if I wear a black polo and some jeans. My wardrobe is tragically unhip at the moment. See you on Saturday @ noon, top of the Met stairs. I can't wait.

-M

S aturday descended onto my life like a Category 6 hurricane. Surviving several wardrobe changes and a few near panic attacks, I found myself racing down East 83rd Street in the direction of the museum. On the phone strapped to my ear was Pippa—an old college roommate and fellow Queens chick—who I deployed as my lifeline in case Marcus turned out to be some psycho killer wrapped in a business school degree. Pippa had many fine qualities, but her memory wasn't one of them. Knowing my friend too well, a last-minute call was in order to remind her of the important girlfriend duties I was depending on.

"You do remember our conversation, right?" I asked, dodging a nanny pushing an oversized stroller. "It was only a couple of days ago."

The brief pause at the end of the line seemed to cement my theory.

"You're going on some sort of blind date, right?"

"Ha, I knew it! Leave it up to you to remember, and I could be chained to a pipe in some foul basement in Jersey right now. Sheesh, so much for getting a little help from my friends. Knowing you, I could remind you and you'd still forget to call."

"Okay, okay. You caught me!" she confessed. "No need to be so dramatic. I said I was going to call. What time do you want me to do this?"

"Two-thirty, three-ish? How long do dates last? It's been so long, I forgot. I *really* hope this one works out. Shit!" I shouted.

Attached to the bottom of my boot heel was a thick, tarry turd—remnants of a dignified furry butthole.

"It's just a date, Kelly, not the end of the world. Nervous, are we?"

"No. Yes. No. Kinda," I stammered, trying to keep my thoughts organized. "I just stepped on a fresh pile of dog shit. Don't these Upper East Siders know how to pick up after their dogs?"

A woman in dark Fendi sunglasses walking a miniature schnauzer shot me a dirty look and zipped by. I sneered back, wondering if that was where the little shit came from.

"They say stepping in dog doody is a good sign," Pippa giggled.

"Maybe in your world, it's definitely not in mine." I dragged my poor boot heal against the concrete curb.

"You sure you aren't nervous? Do you even know what this guy looks like?"

"Of course I'm a little nervous. Who wouldn't be? And no, I don't know what he looks like. But we really clicked. I'd like to think this will be a good match."

"But you've never even seen a picture. You're crazy."

"Why? Looks aren't everything."

"Oh please, Kelly. You would never go out with a guy that looked like Jabba the Hut. Anyway, who goes and meets a total stranger through the Internet? Especially when you haven't seen his face? The whole thing freaks me out."

"Come on, Pippa. It's the year 2000, Y2K never happened. The Internet is safe. Besides, why else am I calling you? Other than your sage criticism, I'm relying on you to be a best friend and make sure I'm not dead? *Hello*, I'm not a total lunatic. You wanna talk crazy? I wasn't the one who had a one-night stand with some weird Serbian guy because he promised to show you his Prince Albert."

"Hey, that was Samantha, not me!" she laughed. "I got stuck with his twin brother—Slavi. He had painted the lyrics to Sweet Child of Mine on his walls with Tide."

"Refresh my memory: Why Tide?"

"Because it glowed in the dark under his black light. At the time I thought it was so cool."

We both belted out a laugh.

"And you still call me nuts," I mused.

"There are a lot of wacka-do's out in the world. You never know what you might find on the computer."

"Online dating can work. I know a girl who met her husband that way. When they got married they gave out little chocolate computers as gifts."

"They sound like dorks," she said.

"They are dorks, but they found love on the Internet. I don't see why I can't either...Look, I'm at the museum. If you don't call and my body is found washed up on Jones Beach— or any other beach for that matter—I'm going to come back and haunt you for the rest of your life. You hear?"

"Don't worry, I promise I'll call. I hope he's as much of a package as he paints himself to be."

"You and me both."

I hung up the phone and looked out over the swathe of yellow taxis overwhelming Fifth Avenue. My eyes scanned up the steps of the Met hoping to catch a glimpse of Marcus, but it was impossible to distinguish anything. People were spread across the gray stone slabs in one large, heaving mass, like a beached whale sucking in its last breaths. Everywhere I looked tourists were snapping pictures and locking lips. At the base of the stairs a large crowd had gathered around a ragtag group of kids breakdancing on a couple of squares of worn cardboard.

I crossed the street, whittling my way around the teeming line of hungry people waiting for their authentic hot dogs, and climbed up the crowded stairs. Before I reached the very top, I did a quick sniff test for potential foul odors. Nothing. Check.

I spotted a speck of shit still clinging to the bottom of my boot heel. *Fucking dogs*, I grumbled. I scraped the heel again while adjusting the shoulder strap of my camo purse so it was visible.

Beneath the waving exhibition banners, I kept a careful eye out for my date. Black polo and jeans, could the man be more nondescript? I popped a slice of gum in my mouth. The warm rush of cinnamon flooded my taste buds and helped soothe the butterflies swarming in my stomach.

Of the solo men with jet-black hair standing around at the top of the stairs, I had narrowed my prospects into two potential candidates. Candidate number one was propped up against the wall, reading a book behind a pair of Ray-Ban sunglasses. His Converse high-tops held up a tall slim frame. He had a pair of well-defined biceps, one of which bore the markings of a Celtic band tattoo peeking from underneath a faded black tee. He radiated a natural cool that instantly had me knock-kneed and tongue-twisted. With one glance, this Hot Toddy had leveled me into a ball of nerves and a pile of drool. If he was Marcus, I swore to God I'd kiss Craig's feet for eternity.

Prospect number two, on the other hand, fell at the opposite end of the spectrum. Instead of exuding a quiet, effortless cool, he was screaming into his cellphone at so high a decibel any eighty year old with a decent ball of earwax would hear the signal loud and clear. His back was turned, so besides the black tee-shirt and jeans, all I could make out was his thick, rounded shoulders and a trail of wispy black hairs attempting to correct a growing bald spot.

Steadfast in my resolve that this was going to be a date I would share with my kids years later, I slapped my eyes shut and beckoned the good vibes to come my way. The meditation came to an abrupt end when Mr. Loud Talker wormed his way into my good-date prayer.

"Nah, bro. Buy low, sell high. Didn't you learn anything in business school? I just sold the last of that shit stock. Company is going belly up any day now. I got a guy who's talking all about this company called 'Google'? Says it's going to reinvent the Internet. Better get in now."

The loud talker was now less than a foot away, pacing back and forth like he was taking a call on the trading floor. Even with his back turned, his voice came in louder than a wind turbine. He loosened the upturned collar of his polo shirt and a nest of black wiry ringlets sprouted around his neck.

I winced. Not only did he have a literal fur collar, but in the right light, his bald spot was the actual size of a dinner plate. There was no way this man could be Marcus, none whatsoever.

I gathered my nerves and turned back around, ready to introduce myself to candidate number one, Mr. Hot Toddy. What I saw wasn't encouraging.

His lips were perched on a skinny blonde whose sinewy arms were latched around his trim waist. *Of course,* I thought, feeling a wee bit deflated. How else could it be? A dude that smokin' doesn't go on blind dates. He probably had more notches on his belt than a train conductor punched holes. Shit, that meant my blind date was either pulling a no-show or Mr. Loud Talker had officially taken the lead.

"Yeah man, I'm out here about to go on a blind date! I don't give a shit about those numbers. Monday morning, I'm going to prove you wrong my friend...."

Fuuuuuuuuuccccccckkk!

I quickly swung my bag around so that it rested against my butt. Maybe I could go inside, pretend I never heard that? As Marcus revealed himself, I realized his hair was the least of his problems. With the exception of his green eyes, he had lied on all fronts of his physical description. He was as short as a fifth grader, while sporting a spare tire and the wrinkles of a forty-year-old. Keanu Reeves my ass, this guy was Bilbo Baggins!

I didn't know what to do. I was trapped in a moral conundrum: Run like hell or do the right thing. The truth was I never was good at being mean. Ditching out now would give me guilt-induced agita for weeks. I reminded myself looks weren't everything and decided to do the mature thing. Perhaps there was still potential for this date somewhere, if I squinted really hard and tried to find it.

"Marcus?" I ask as I tapped him on the shoulder.

"Gotta go," he shouted into the phone and slapped it shut. His peridot colored eyes honed in on my bag. His puffy lips curled into a wide grin.

"Kelly, so nice to finally meet you," he said, lowering his voice an octave for the special occasion.

I forced a smile. "The one and only...I hope you weren't waiting too long. I had some train trouble."

"Nah, just a couple of minutes. Gorgeous day, isn't it? What a great idea to come here. I could sit out here and people watch for hours. There are a lot of characters on these steps."

You could say that again, I thought. "So, are you ready to see some mummies?"

"With you milady, any day. Lead the way."

I bit my tongue and led us inside to the museum's cavernous marble lobby. While Marcus marched up to the booth to buy our tickets, I wondered what else in his profile would amount to a pile of steaming horse turds. A second later he returned with two pink metal tabs with an M in the middle. He pinned one on my collar.

"I tried to get them to give me a color that would match your pretty eyes, but all they had was this bubble gum pink. Sorry, it was the best I could do."

Ok, that was sweet, I thought. Maybe I was being too hasty. Anger was never a good feeling to take on a first date. From that moment on, I decided to let it all go and give Marcus a proper chance. I thanked him for the compliment and together we walked through the crowds into the Egyptian wing.

Over the glass display cases filled with colorful beaded jewelry and mummified remains, we swapped stories about life and travel. I talked about my life growing up in New York City and exploring European capitals. He spoke of his backpack adventures through Southeast Asia. While I sipped wine in Paris, he was slurping noodles in Thailand.

We followed the steady stream of people into the Sackler Gallery—a sunlit room, lined with glass panels overlooking Central Park. Outside the trees were blooming with white budding flowers. Springtime in the park was always a pretty thing.

We took a seat beside a reflective pool filled with papyrus plants and stared at the Temple of Dendur, a two-thousand-year-old sandstone structure carved with hieroglyphics depicting Julius Caesar's son as a pharaoh.

"So, how do you like New York so far?" I asked.

"It's different than Cambridge, that's for sure. Harvard Business School didn't give me an opportunity to see much of Boston. I was either too busy studying or too tired to do anything else. In terms of New York, I like what I see so far."

His fluorescent green eyes stared at me with such intent, I wanted to squirm. Was he wearing colored contacts? I couldn't tell and feared an extensive eye examination would spur him on even more. So I did the dainty thing—blushed and turned away.

"Do you want to have kids?" he asked in an attempt to break the awkward silence.

"Um, I guess. I'm certainly not in a hurry. You?"

"One day, definitely. Sooner than later is my way of thinking. I'm not trying to have them too late. I've got the whole thing worked out."

"Really?"

"Oh, yeah. I'm going to do it exactly the way my parents did it with me. Have kids on the earlier side, if possible of course"—he smiled—"and when they're six or seven, send them to boarding school."

"Boarding school? That's a little early don't you think?"

"That's the age I was shipped off."

"Seriously? Shipped off. What were you? Cargo?"

"Something like that. Awful sounding, I know, but rest assured it wasn't as bad as I'm painting it. My parents sent me to a nice, proper school in the Swiss Alps. Hardly a prison. Going to boarding school is what kids of diplomats do."

"Wow. That is certainly not how I imagine raising children. Call me crazy, but I want to be around to raise my kids."

"What for?" he laughed. "You enjoy them so much more on holidays. Believe me, I didn't mind being away, and I'm sure neither did my parents."

"Well, the furthest away I got from my parents was eight weeks of summer camp. That's what city kids do. Our parents sent us to the hills for some greenery and fresh air. Otherwise, we'd get into a lot of trouble. It has something to do with the summer's sticky heat. Kid's get a little cuckoo. But getting dumped in the Berkshires isn't half as far as Switzerland."

"Did you attend public or private school?" His voice was tentative.

"Public."

"I see." He munched on the side of his mouth, trying to mask his disappointment.

"Why? Amazed I turned out so cultured?"

Now it was his turn to squirm.

"No, no. I didn't mean it that way, not really," he stammered. "I'm sure the New York public school system has a lot to offer..."

"Alright, now I know you are full of it!" I said half-joking. "You're trying to figure out if I'd fit into your upper-crust environs. I see how it is."

His cheeks flushed but he didn't acknowledge it. "Okay, let's switch gears. I don't know about you, but I'm hungry. I spotted a diner on my way over here. What do you say we ditch the dead people and grab some lunch? My treat."

I cocked a surly smile. "Trying to get out of sounding like an elitist snob?"

"Perhaps, but I am pretty hungry and not willing to give up on this date yet." He stood up, extended a hand and pulled me to my feet. "Besides, I like it when a woman calls me out like that."

Oh, the poor soul; if he only knew the half.

In the end, I agreed to lunch because I didn't know how to say no. Those two little letters were my Achilles heel and it would take years before I learned how to use them well. If I'd had the courage to say no more often, I probably could've spared myself endless nights babysitting cranky kids, getting achy arms from helping people move, or—like today—lingering too long on a date that had long passed its expiration date.

The diner Marcus had mentioned was a discreet eatery tucked between a jewelry store for six-figure bank accounts and a Parisian children's boutique on fashionable Madison Avenue. If it weren't for the mirrored walls and the aroma of fresh brewed coffee, I would have mistaken the place for another high-end retailer for upper-crusters. Instead of taking the cozy back booth Marcus had his eye on, I suggested a small, non-romantic table in the center of the room. Over the clinking plates and muffled street noise, a thick-soled waitress dropped a couple of menus on the table and prattled off a list of the day's specials. She gave us a couple of minutes to decide and filled up our glasses with ice water. No sooner had I checked time on the fifties-style wall clock, my cellphone started ringing. It was Pippa calling to check in.

"Hi Mom," I winked at Marcus as I answered the phone.

"Soooo?" Pippa hummed. "You're obviously alive. Still on the date?"

"Yup."

"Going good?"

"No...I can't chat right now. Can I call you back later? I'm out to lunch."

"Lunch? The date can't be going that bad."

"I wouldn't be so sure of that." I looked over at Marcus. He had both menus in his hand and was in a heated discussion with the waitress over a few select items.

"I know you can't talk but you gotta give me something. Is he cute at least?"

"The furthest thing from."

"Ha! I told you these things never work out."

"Thanks Mom, you're the best. Look, I got to go. Talk to you later..."

"I ordered for the both of us. I hope you don't mind," Marcus said as I put away my phone. "I thought a round of apple martinis and couple turkey club sandwiches should hit the spot."

"Apple martinis: your favorite," I noted. "I'm surprised they make them here."

"They don't. But they know me here." He flashed me a smile, looking pretty pleased with himself.

On cue, the waitress set down two martini glasses filled to the rim with a glowing green liquid. He tapped the rim of my glass and took a big gulp.

"Did you special-order the turkey too?" I asked.

"No, no. I'm on a health kick and the only thing I eat these days is turkey. I'm trying to get back to my fighting weight. These desk jobs are a killer on my waistline." He slapped his belly. "You like running?"

"Not really." I took a sip of the martini. It was so cloying my lips puckered. I settled it back down on the table. "I was never really good at it."

"No one is *bad* at running. On our next date, I'll take you for a jog around the park. Maybe you'll let me change your mind."

A second date? What was he, nuts? He was lucky he'd gotten me this far. I was ready to bolt before we hit the starting gate. A second round was not going to happen. No, the kibosh needed to be put on this date before things turned ugly.

"Out of curiosity, what sign are you?" I asked.

"You mean, astrology?"

"Yeah. Depending on your sign, you prefer different sports. Like, Pisces is a water sign, and they do well swimming. I'm guessing you're an Aries."

The look on his face told me we were entering foreign waters. This was exactly where I wanted him to be.

"I was born in April. What sign is that?"

"As I thought: you're an Aries."

"Huh." He leaned back and watched the turkey club sandwiches arrive at the table. "You believe in that stuff?"

"Astrology...tarot cards...palm reading...I live for it. Ever since I was a little girl, I was super drawn to it. I think it had something to do with the ghost that lived in my apartment."

Marcus, who had his head buried in his sandwich, looked up in disbelief. It was working. I kept going.

"I know it sounds crazy, but I swear there was an actual ghost that lived in my building. We had all these strange things happening in the apartment."

"What kind of strange things?" His voice was hesitant, as if he didn't like where this was heading.

"You know, the stereotypical stuff: Lights flickering; sounds of footsteps even though I was home alone. Sometimes there were weird smells, like the kind you'd find in a church."

"Incense?"

"Exactly! At first I thought I was imagining things, but after I found out the same stuff was happening to my downstairs neighbor, I knew our building was haunted. That's how I fell into Wicca."

" 'Wicca'?" He took another hard gulp of his apple martini. Nothing was left except the lone maraschino cherry sitting at the bottom of the glass. "Now you're going have to help me out on this one. What is 'Wicca'?"

"Oh come on, you lived in Massachusetts. I'm sure you learned all about the Salem witch hunts."

"You're telling me you're a witch? Are you serious?"

"Well you don't have to say it like it's a dirty word. Wicca is a legitimate religion."

Now I had him by the balls and wasn't going to let go until he was ready to run for the hills. Considering the way he was plowing through his food and drink, I figured we were almost there.

"So then what do you guys do, cast spells using chickens? You've got to be messing with me."

I assured him I was not by detailing the finer points of the religion. I explained chickens were used with voodoo and black magic. To be a Wiccan was to be peaceful and good. It was about being one with nature. We weren't allowed to hurt animals; it went against the whole principle of Wiccan belief.

I had to give it to Marcus: he sat staring at me without a hint of judgment, only a look of wonderment. A few minutes later and he was scratching a hole in his bald spot, trying to figure out how this date had gone so wonderfully wrong.

"My coven gets together once a month and we do spells for all sorts of things. Like for instance, the day before we met online, I burned a spell candle for love and look who it led me to—you!"

"Wow, isn't that amazing." He shoved the last piece of turkey into his mouth.

From across the table I watched him wriggle in his chair so badly, crossing and uncrossing his legs, that I had to keep talking for fear I'd bust out laughing and blow my own cover.

"I know all this is a lot to take in. It took me a bit of time to process how the universe works. See, it wasn't fate that brought us together. It was the Goddess. She saw the light in my candle and answered my prayers."

"You're finished eating, right? I think I'll just get us the check." Marcus's frantic eyes flagged down the waitress and he motioned for the bill. He stared down at his watch a little longer than normal, like he was calculating the time zones we just passed. "Damn, you know I didn't realize how late it was. I forgot I am supposed to be back at my apartment in twenty minutes."

I feigned disappointment. "Really? Oh, that's too bad. I was having such a nice time."

"Yeah, me too. It's nothing personal, you know. It's one of those business things—a conference call."

"On a Saturday?"

"Asian markets. They're open six days a week."

"Huh. I never knew that."

"Not many people do," he said, and diverted his attention to the bill.

We agreed to go Dutch. It was twenty bucks even. Afterwards, Marcus and I walked to the subway. Normally this would be our chance to part ways and never see each other again, but as it turned out both of us were heading in the same direction. Lucky for Marcus, we had a few more minutes to spend together.

As the Number 6 train barreled downtown, I spent our last precious moments together carefully laying out ideas for our next date: rollerblading, bowling, a coven session maybe...

With each suggestion I made, Marcus moved an inch closer towards the exit. By the time the train pulled into his station, his back was suction-cupped to the door. I took advantage of the situation and planted a fat wet goodbye kiss on his cheek. He followed it up with a handshake.

"It was nice meeting you," he said.

"So next weekend? Maybe we should do that run in the park like you suggested? I'll wear something bright and tight," I winked.

"Yeah, um...Let's talk. I gotta check my work schedule. I'll get back to you. It was a pleasure, really it was. Here's my stop. Gotta run!"

And run he did. He charged up the stairs without looking back.

I guess there is such a thing as magic after all.

posted: 2002-02-19 9:27am EDT

$2150/Totally stunning pre-war 1 bdrm Apt in heart of Greenwich Village. Hurry up—a deal this good won't last!!!

Gorgeous 1 bedroom apartment you must see to believe! Located walking distance to Washington Square Park, it's perfect for professionals or mature college students. The newly renovated property has hardwood floors, a working fireplace, and access to a communal rooftop garden. It also boosts 12 ft ceilings and all new stainless steel appliances.

Call today for viewing.
Simply the Best Apts @ (212) 439-5555.

- cats are OK, purr
- dogs are OK, woof
- Location: GREENWICH VILLAGE near A/B/C/E/F/V trains
- It's NOT okay to solicit this person with services or other unrelated interests
- Listed by: Simply the Best Apts

All Apartments

Historians say September 11, 2001 changed the world forever. It certainly did for me. After those two hijacked planes slammed into the Twin Towers, I lost my job to a jittery economy. You could say losing an income was a different kind of casualty.

Times were rough in the city; people lost loved ones, businesses collapsed, daily bomb scares brought commuters to their knees. While you could turn off the television, there was no escape from the smell of underground fires, or from hushed conspiracy theories. And yet despite the sorrows and setbacks, resolve was strong in the city. There was all this talk of rebuilding, renewing, and getting our lives back to normal. Funny thing, I didn't want to go back to normal; getting laid off was the best thing that could have happened to me.

I had grown tired of working for shitty magazines and hiding from bipolar bosses in cubicle settings. I wanted to be my own boss, set my own hours, be outside, take lunch breaks at three if it pleased me. The idea was to get into real estate.

If I had consulted my magic eight ball it would have told me "Outlook not so good" and to "Try again later." But I was a tough nut and determined to make real estate my business. Shit, I was personal, cute enough, and a decent salesperson—I knew I could make this work. I took the ten-hour course, got my license, and nabbed a gig at Simply the Best Apartments, a new real-estate kid on the block who was plucking up newly minted agents faster than cops spat out parking tickets. Pippa joined in on the adventure, and together we became part of the Simply the Best family.

At the helm of this ship was a man named Harold Goldstein. He was a short, pudgy Jewish guy from downtown Brooklyn. He had pot-marked skin, wore pants too big, and had a permanent string of white spittle that liked to bounce between his lips each time he opened his mouth to speak. He ran his empire from a floor-through loft on 23rd Street in Chelsea. The loft was set up like a trading floor and agents got to choose their desks from long rows of folding tables. Each space had a computer to search through the company's database of listings, and if we wanted, we could print our own business cards.

Pippa and I chose to keep up a professional decorum by choosing seats on opposite sides of the room. But any chance we got we were calling each other on the phone, gossiping about the last shitbox we had just shown. See, Simply the Best had a policy that agents were not allowed to preview apartments before showing them to clients. Harold thought it would make us better sales agents. So on this particular day, as I waited for my four o'clock to arrive, I answered the phone and got a guy requesting the most talked-about dump in the office.

"I'm calling about the studio apartment in Murray Hill," bellowed the gruff male voice.

"Okay, let me look that up for you." I tapped away at the computer and found about a dozen listings for studio apartments in the Murray Hill area. But I knew instinctively which one he was going for—the cheapest. "We've got a number of apartments available. Were you interested in the twelve-hundred dollar one?"

"That's it. Says it's got wood floors and popcorn-sprayed ceilings. What the hell are popcorn-sprayed ceilings?"

"I believe it means sprayed-on stucco. Think textured."

"Are there closets? If I'm going to squeeze into a studio, I've got to have a place to hide my things."

"Closet space shouldn't be a problem. Would you like to make an appointment and come in, so we can see the space?"

Another of Harold's policies was to bring clients into the office before taking them out for viewings. The idea was to get the client to fill out our three-page renter profile questionnaire and inadvertently sign off on our agent fee—fifteen percent of the annual rent.

"How about we just meet at the apartment instead? My time is limited."

"See, I'd love to do that, but it's Simply the Best's policy to meet here first. I know it's a pain. Trust me, you'll forget all about that once you see the apartment. You're going to love it, I promise."

"That sounds all nice and sweet hon, but I'm a *very* busy man with a lot of important meetings to keep."

This was coming from a man who was looking at the smallest and cheapest listing we offered.

"You want to see the apartment, you need to come in. Company policy," I insisted.

"Did you hear about the real-estate agent that got bludgeoned to death while showing an apartment?"

"Excuse me?"

"Happened the other day. Got her face all smashed in by a sledgehammer," he said without a hint of sympathy. "Did you hear about it?"

"No, I didn't. That kind of stuff doesn't scare me."

"Maybe, it should. You go around, meeting strangers all day. You never know what could happen. New York is a dangerous city."

"I carry a Taser," I said, sensing it was time to hang up the phone.

"Now that's interesting. Pretty wild stuff, those Tasers. Where'd you learn how to shoot one of those things?"

"The Discovery Channel," I said. "Look, someone's on my line. It's time I go."

"What about the apartment? When can I take a look at it? Bring your Taser along. We can have fun together."

"In your dreams, freak."

I slammed down the phone, just in time for my four o'clock's arrival.

At the front desk, Molly, the third receptionist to be hired during my short tenure, was directing a twenty-something Asian guy in a hoodie towards my desk. I flipped open my Filofax in a vain attempt to look professional, and read the scribbled notes:

Allen?? Looking for 1 bdroom in Village.
Called about $2150 near Washington Square Park

I mentally brushed off the grime from that last caller and got into a go-get-em' frame of mind. Truth was, I was entering my fourth week at Simply the Best and had zero to show for it. My bank account was in double digits. I needed to land a rental soon or I'd be out on the street.

When the client arrived I stood up and extended my hand. "Hi Allen, I'm Kelly. Nice to meet you, finally. Please sit down." I offered him a seat and slid a clipboard in his direction. "Just answer the questions and sign your name at the last page—it's nothing, just a waiver. When you're done, we'll go through the database and get you into some apartments today."

I could feel Harold's beady eyes watching me from the other end of the loft. He tapped on his computer screen with a chipped fingernail. I suppressed an eye roll and flicked on my monitor. On the screen a bold headline appeared: *Raising the rent on no-fee apartments in wake of 9/11*. It was a bogus promotional piece written by a scummy real estate developer looking to minimize his loss in Manhattan's freefalling rental market. According to Harold's rulebook of sleazy sale tactics, all Simply the Best Apartments employees were required to have the article on display for our client's pleasure reading. Recently, I got caught turning off the monitor during a meeting and now I was a red flag on Harold's radar screen.

After Allen diligently filled out the questionnaire, we assessed his likes and needs and narrowed our search down to three apartments—three being the magic number. The rule was to show them three places. Start with the cheapest and most dingy, and work your way up. The first on the list was a basement studio apartment with a view of the building's air-conditioning vents. The apartment had been on the market for over a year, and not even the slickest, sell-ice-to-an-Eskimo salesman was able to move it. It was a long shot at best.

"So, what do you think?" I asked as I turned on the overhead lights.

The studio was darker than a coal mine, muggy, and totally devoid of charm. Allen gave it a quick look around and shook his head. In less than two minutes we were out the door and on to our next stop: A sunny junior-four apartment with a decorative fireplace and original wooden floors. Taking the cues from Harold's playbook, I assured Allen the next place promised to be much better despite the slightly higher price tag.

"The landlord said he was upgrading the common areas this year. So just ignore all the mess," I chuckled, as we crossed the cracked-tile threshold and into the five-story walk up on Sullivan Street.

"It's all good," he said. "Places like this don't faze me. I'm from New York."

"Oh, yeah? Me too. What parts?" I asked, trying to ignore the carcasses of dead water bugs, strewn about the old marble steps like a trail of squashed raisins.

"Really, you look like you're from Massachusetts or Cali. Aren't all real estate agents from out of town?"

"Not this one."

"Originally I'm from Flushing, but I'm staying at my parent's place in Staten Island. I gotta get the hell outta there."

We swerved around another fluorescent-lit landing and got smacked in the face with the scent of curried lamb.

"Look, I'm going to level with you," I said, overcome with the urge to come clean about Harold's scheme. "You seem like a nice guy and I don't want to jerk you around. Truth is I haven't seen this place. But from the looks of it, I have the feeling it's going to be another dump."

"It can't be that bad. I don't see crack vials around," Allen laughed. "Thanks for the honesty. How many floors up is it?"

"Only four more, I hope you ate your power breakfast."

By the time we reached the fifth floor my legs felt like they were ready to collapse. While Allen caught his breath, I wrangled the key from my purse in front of a thickly painted metal door with a protruding fish-angle peep hole. Above the old brass knob were seven different locks running the length of the door. I slipped my key at the newest lock at the top and the door growled open. We stepped inside and I cringed. The apartment looked like the stage of a grisly, unsolved murder mystery.

Every inch of the five-hundred square foot apartment was covered in a thick black mold. Chunks of sheetrock were missing from the ceiling—the result of an ongoing water leak. The "European-style" kitchenette was nothing more than a greasy hotplate propped on top of an old phone book. In the corner was a stained porcelain sink and a mini fridge filled with rotting food from the previous owner. Even the decorative fireplace was filthy, its mantle boarded up with rotting plywood. I looked around for a selling point and was hard pressed to find one.

"Well, at least some of the walls are the original brick," I said.

"What a shithole!" Allen yelped. "I wondered what happened in here."

"Yo, bro—you don't want this place," said a guy standing at the open door. His head was shaved and he wore a pair of black combat boots. Half of his arm was covered in a Darth Vader tattoo.

I gave him a once over. "And who are you?"

"Name's Franky. I live next door. Trust me—I wouldn't be coming over here if I didn't think people ought to know."

"Ought to know what? That you're looking to expand? Is that it?"

Franky smirked and propped his arm against the door. "Expand into this dump? Shit, honey—my crib ain't a looker, but *hell* no, I won't be stepping a toe in there."

"Why? You know something?" Allen asked.

"Shit man, don't you feel it? This place is straight-up haunted."

Allen and I looked around the room and then towards each other.

"So a guy died in here," I said. "Big deal. I could show you a dozen other places where that's happened. This is New York, a big city. People die."

"People don't die like this guy." Frankie swiped his thumb across his nose. "Homeboy was murdered."

Great. If that wouldn't kill a rental deal, I don't know what would. "Alright, time to go, Allen." The apartment and its chatty neighbor were beginning to give me the creeps.

"Hold up," Allen said. Then he turned back to Franky. "For real? Murdered?"

"Cops said he was stabbed...*anally*." Franky winced. "Shit ain't right."

"Oh good lord," I cried out. "*Now* can we leave?"

"Wait a minute...No fucking way. I can't believe it." Allen repeated his disbelief over and over again. "I've never been in a place where someone was murdered before. No wonder this place looks straight out of a horror movie."

"I told you people, you don't want to be up in here."

As much as I tried urging Allen to get out of there, he stood fixated on Franky, thoroughly intrigued. "You heard it happening? Did you call the police?"

"Hell, no! I was at my girl's place at the time. When I came back, there was a godawful stank in the hallway. The whole building was stinkin'! My peeps stopped rolling through because of that shit. It took a month for it to get real bad. That's when the old lady, Mrs. P., on the second floor, called it in. Homeboy died a true New York City death."

Franky made it sound like the death was heroic.

Allen was so riveted by the grim tale that for a split second I thought about working the angle; then my moral compass took over. I headed towards the door; I'd heard way more than I ever needed to hear.

"Okay, I'm out of here," I said. "Don't think I need to know any more about this place."

"Good girl," Franky snapped back as I squeezed between him and the door.

I sucked my teeth. I never understood why men made comments like that, as if all women were wild horses needing taming? I glanced back at my client, who was soaking up everything we'd just heard. "Allen? Are you coming?"

He took one last look around and followed me into the hallway. Franky gave him a fist pump. I said nothing and headed down the stairs.

Outside Allen asked, "How much are they asking for that place?"

"Two thousand and some serious bragging rights. Why, you're interested? Maybe I should get that guy to help me rent places. He certainly adds flair to the business."

"Chill, I got enough problems with nosey neighbors. My mom is one of 'em. So how many more places are you taking me to? Just wondering if I need to be packing heat."

I laughed. "We've got one more. Think you can handle it?"

"There's only one way to find out."

We walked down Sullivan Street and took a short cut through Washington Square Park. Underneath the old oak trees hustlers played speed chess. The old dried up fountain was filled with the dangling legs of NYU kids. Every few seconds a skateboard would slap its dirt-covered wheels against the pavement. The homeless and the drunk wandered past us with paper coffee cups and outstretched hands begging for change—penny, nickel, dime, quarter. On occasion, one of them would ask us if we wanted some ecstasy.

Allen pulled out a pack of Newport Lights from his back pocket and offered me one. I knew it was unprofessional, but I sure as hell needed a cigarette. Franky's story was still fresh on the brain and the smoke felt good.

"Too bad they don't make these things stronger," I said. "I'd love to erase all memory of that last place."

"That can be arranged. We are in Washington Square Park after all." He smiled.

"You might not be working right now, but I am! Oh look, we're almost here."

We slipped out of the park and crossed the block onto Waverly Place—a sliver of a street lined with brick townhouses, flower boxes, and shuttered windows. Once we got to the address, I instructed Allen to hang out on the stoop while I retrieved the keys from the below-ground office. At the door I was greeted by a crotchety guy who pointed me in the direction of two middle-aged Hasidic men having lunch. In their hands were a couple of shawarmas swaddled in yogurt and tinfoil. One of the men ignored me and kept eating. The other set his food aside, wiped his fingers against his dark wool pants and walked over to an old medicine cabinet filled with keys.

"I don't know why you people keep asking for the key. You are supposed to have it." His voice had the hint of an Eastern European accent.

"I'm sorry, I don't know anything about that," I said. "I'll ask around when I go back."

"What building you want?"

"The one upstairs: 17 Waverley. Apartment 204 I believe."

He slipped on a pair of reading glasses and checked the tags, one by one. "I don't see it here. You must have it."

"I know I don't have it. I checked before I came out here. Look—my client is waiting outside, can you please look again? It's got to be here."

He grumbled something indistinguishable and continued looking. Eventually, he found it hanging in a place where it shouldn't have been. "If your company took better care, I wouldn't have to interrupt my lunch and look for keys all day." He pushed the set into my palm. "Make sure you give it back when you are done. You understand?"

I gave him a quick nod and ran up the stairs.

Once on the street, I was struck by something odd. There was a cop car sitting half up on the sidewalk with its red lights twirling. What was going on? Where was Allen? I scratched my head and looked at the stairs where I last left him.

Out of nowhere a meat locker of a man approached me. He was wearing a pair of wraparound shades and had a police badge dangling from his thick neck.

"Excuse me miss," he asked. "You know this guy?"

He stepped aside and thumbed over to Allen, whose arms were behind his back. I was in shock.

"Allen? What the—"

"Miss, I'm going have to ask you again—do you know this individual?"

A surge of nerves flew right through me. I looked at Allen and then to the cop. "I guess so. I'm his real estate agent."

"Well, you aren't going to be renting him an apartment today." The cop nodded to his partner, who slapped a pair of handcuffs on Allen's wrist. "Put him in the back. We'll go ahead and take him down to central booking."

I looked towards Allen for some answers. "What happened? I was only gone for a minute."

All I got out of Allen was a shrug of the shoulders before he was shoved in the back of the squad car.

"Your client was stupid. We caught him out here rolling a joint," said the cop. "Last week we did a sweep in this building and arrested a ring of guys cooking up PCP. They had turned one of the apartments into a full-fledged lab. We gotta make sure your client isn't in the system."

"Oh come on, look at him," I pleaded. "He lives with his parents in Staten Island. Officer please, he's not part of some drug ring. He's just a regular guy who made a stupid mistake."

"Doesn't matter. He was about to smoke weed. It wasn't his lucky day."

"But it's Friday. He's going to be in there all weekend."

"Not my problem and it shouldn't be yours either. If I were you, I'd stay away from people like him."

"If you think he's bad, you should've seen the last guy I just spoke with."

"Perhaps it's time for a new job."

"Maybe you're right."

The cop stuffed his beefy body into the passenger side of the squad car and slammed the door shut. His partner flicked on the siren and the megaphone heaved out a loud whoop. As I watched the car roll off the curb and take off down the block, Allen turned his head towards me. I made the phone sign with my hand and shouted, "Call me when you get out."

posted: 2004-06-11 12:23 pm EDT

Laptop for sale!

Selling my Toshiba Satellite A-75. Moving soon, need to get rid of excess!

The computer is less than a year old. It has a Pentium 4 processor, Windows operating system, and Microsoft Office (WordPerfect, Excel, Powerpoint etc.) 15.4 inch screen, CD/DVD drive. 512 MB of RAM and 60GB Harddrive. Minor scratches on one corner, but in otherwise perfect condition. Asking $400 AC/Adapter included. Serious inquiries only. No scams please.

- Location: New York
- It's NOT okay to solicit this person with services or other unrelated interests

All for Sale

From: Miss Cece Browne <Ccbebe66@yahoo.com>
To: zqrfc-7552912026@sale.cl.org
Date: June 14, 2004 3:37a.m.

Subject: Laptop for Sale

Hello!

Greetings. Hope you doing well today. I will be very interested in your laptop. My boss sey the computer is perfect for my job but he be responsible for paying so I must send you check for $1500 before, ok. So he sey he will issue you check for $1500. When you receive check, you take the $400 and send my boss back the rest $1100. I travel for work now, and the money he get back ($1100) will pay for me to get back home to my children. OK so he seys he going to send check today.

If you kindly please give to me:
You FULL NAME
You CONTAKT ADRESS
You PHONE # and COUNTY CODE

Please my boss sey he want to buy computer now so I can go home. I look forward to hear from you SOON! Tank you well!

Cece Browne

Wow, holy scam. I love messing with these people. Ms.Cece didn't know it yet, but she was about to be a well of entertainment. I sent her back the following message:

From: Kelly B <kellyb@hotmail.com>
To: Miss Cece Browne <Ccbebe66@yahoo.com>
Date: June 14, 2004 6:56 p.m.

Re: Laptop for Sale

Hello Cece,

Thank you for your interest in my laptop. I'm sure you and your boss will be happy with it. Here is my contact info for you to send your check:

Kelly Babar
GoldFinger Productions LLC.
99 Box Street Suite#7
Brooklyn, N.Y. 11222

As soon as I receive your check, I will notify you.

Best regards,
Kelly

From: Miss Cece Browne
To: Kelly B <kellyb@hotmail.com>
Date: June 15, 2004 2:09 a.m.

Re: Laptop for Sale

Greetings Miss Kelly,

I hope you are doing good today. I spoke with my boss and he
seys he put check in mail today. So check you post because
you will receive check in a few days. Ok, tank you.

Have good day,
Cece Browne

From: Kelly B
To: Miss Cece Browne <Ccbebe66@yahoo.com>
Date: June 24, 2004 10:29 a.m.

Re: Laptop for Sale

Hi Cece,

I received your boss's check today 6/22/2004 for $1500.
The check says it's from Qchex.com. I looked for a
watermark but I could not find one. Plus, the check appears
to be printed on regular copy paper? Before I go ahead and
deposit this, can you please check with your boss that the
check is authentic?

Thanks,
Kelly

Re: Laptop for Sale

Hello Kelly,

Greetings! I hope all is today well. I spoke with my boss and he seys the check is autenthicated. So you may please go and put check in you bank account, ok?

Tank you!
Cece

I let the issue sit for a few days, wondering how Cece might react under the pressure. A week later, I received this email:

From: **Miss Cece Browne**
To: Kelly B <kellyb@hotmail.com>
Date: July 2, 2004 1:12 a.m.

Re: Laptop for Sale

Hello Kelly,

This Cece. I still waiting and hear no word about check. Ok, I hope you is doing well. Please tell me you deposit check and I can tell my boss because he want the laptop. Tank you.

Love,
Cece

She was so close to finishing her scam, I could almost smell her desperation. I wanted to throw her off course a little, so I offered up this carrot.

From: **Allie Baba** <ababa76@hotmail.com>
To: Miss Cece Browne <Ccbebe66@yahoo.com>
Date: July 5, 2004 9:03 a.m.

Re: Laptop for Sale

Hello Cece,

I am Kelly's office assistant, Allie. She spoke with me about the check, and apologizes for the delay—she's away on business at the moment. She assured me the check was deposited last week, before her trip.

I understand there is a difference of $1100. What would you like me to do with the remaining? Once the check clears, I will ship the laptop to you.

Sorry for the inconvenience.

Take care,
Ms. Allie Baba

From: Miss Cece Browne
To: Allie Baba <ababa76@hotmail.com>
Date: July 6, 2004 3:03 a.m.

Re: Laptop for Sale

Greetings Miss Allie Baba,

Please I like you to wire money to my boss. Once he recieve money, then I give you address to send you the laptop to him. Now I can go home to my tree children. God bless. It been too long time that I am away from my family.

Ok so you wire money trough MONEYGRAM. Ok. You do it today, yes!

SHOLA ADENIJI
36 BISHOP OLUWOLE
VICTORIA ISLAND
ETI-OSA
LAGOS
NIGERIA
12999

Please you wire MONEYGRAM today ok?

Tanks,
Cece

From: Allie Baba
To: Miss Cece Browne <Ccbebe66@yahoo.com>
Date: July 5, 2004 9:03 a.m.

Re: Laptop for Sale

Hi Cece,

I have sent the $1100 via Moneygram to the information you sent above:

Shola Adeniji, 36 Bishop Oluwole, Victoria Island, Eti-Osa, Lagos, Nigeria, 12999.
Reference #MG27H9478.
The sender's name: Allie Baba.

Please let me know when you collect the money. I know Kelly really wants you to have the laptop.

Have a great day,
Allie

From: Miss Cece Browne
To: Allie Baba <ababa76@hotmail.com>
Date: July 6, 2004 2:52 a.m.

Re: Laptop for Sale

Miss Allie,
Tank you for sending the money but my boss seys money no there. You sent the correct #? Ok, so you get back to me soon,

ok? It is very URGENT because my boss need your computer for work.

God bless,
Cece

Okay, now we're getting somewhere! Time to turn on the heat...

From: Allie Baba
To: Miss Cece Browne <Ccbebe66@yahoo.com>
Date: July 6, 2004 9:43 a.m.

Re: Laptop for Sale

Hi Cece,

I'm so sorry. It's funny because I am pretty sure the confirmation number I sent you is correct. The confirmation number is **#MG27H9478**. Try again, I promise the money is there.

Allie

From: Miss Cece Browne
To: Allie Baba <ababa76@hotmail.com>
Date: July 7, 2004 4:51 a.m.

Re: Laptop for Sale

Miss Allie,

I went again to Moneygram. They seys the confirmation number is 10 numbers! My boss really need laptop and I need to go home to my family. Please, please check the number ok?
God bless,
Cece

From: Allie Baba
To: Miss Cece Browne <Ccbebe66@yahoo.com>
Date: July 7, 2004 10:22 a.m.

Re: Laptop for Sale

Oh my gosh, I am soooo sorry Cece!!! I double checked the confirmation number and you were right—I was missing a few numbers. I don't know how I could have done that! I'm so silly sometimes. Please, don't mention this to my boss. Kelly would kill me if she found out.

So here is the new confirmation number: #MG27H94781127

Have a great day!
Allie B.

From: Miss Cece Browne
To: Allie Baba <ababa76@hotmail.com>
Date: July 7, 2004 1:04 a.m.

Re: Laptop for Sale

Hello,

Miss Allie please you again send me wrong number!!! I went to Moneygram and lady there seys she going to call police. Police sey they will arrest me! Please this very urgent!!! My baby is sick, and my boss seys he won't buy me ticket with no money and laptop.

Ok, so you get bak to me please.

God Bless,
Cece

Whoops! Looks like Cece Brown is sweating bullets. This is so much better than toying with telemarketers! I wanted to ride this wave until she couldn't keep up.

From: Allie Baba
To: Miss Cece Browne <Ccbebe66@yahoo.com>
Date: July 8, 2004 4:13 p.m.

Re: Laptop for Sale

Cece,

Did you say Moneygram? No wonder the confirmation number won't work! I sent the money through UPS. I feel so bad. I beg you, can we keep this between ourselves? If Kelly finds out that I messed this up, she will fire me. I've only been working here for three months. I'd hate to look for another job.

Thank you so much for your discretion. I really appreciate it. Here is the new number: 10824261903

Email me as soon as you get the money. I would really like to send out this laptop before Kelly gets back from her trip. I wish your baby gets better soon!

All the best,
Allie

From: Miss Cece Browne
To: Allie Baba <ababa76@hotmail.com>
Date: July 9, 2004 3:01 a.m.

Re: Laptop for Sale

Miss Allie, I don't know what game you play. Today, I went to UPS they seys you numbre is wrong again! My boss seys he want laptop and won't send me home until $1100 go trough. My baby is very very sick.

Ok, send me correct # and I no say nothing to Miss Kelly.

This Cece, ok.

From: Miss Cece Browne
To: Kelly B <kellyb@hotmail.com>
Date: July 9, 2004 3:12 a.m.

Re: Laptop for Sale

Hello Miss Kelly,

This is Cece, you remember me? You assistant Allie suppose to send me $1100 to my boss for laptop. She give me tree wrong number already!!! I want you to know Allie is no doing her job very good.

God Bless,
Cece

From: Allie Baba
To: Miss Cece Browne <Ccbebe66@yahoo.com>
Date: July 11, 2004 9:15 a.m.

Re: Laptop for Sale

Hi Cece,

I checked with UPS first thing this morning and this is the reference number they gave me: 1082426190378921 1XHM
Have a great day!
Allie

P.S. Thanks so much for not saying anything to Kelly. She seems to be in a good mood this morning :)

P.P.S. Hope your baby is feeling better!

To: Allie Baba <ababa76@hotmail.com>
Date: July 11, 2004 11:49 p.m.

Re: Laptop for Sale

Miss Allie,

I no understand you. UPS peeple seys number no correct. AGAIN!!! They call police, I run out before they come! I beginging to tink you are a really bad worker. Miss Kelly will hear about tis I promise, ok?

My boss is very mad. He need $1100 to bring me home and he want laptop for work. My baby feeling very bad. I need go home soon. Please, you send me correct number now. OK????!!!!

Cece

Boy, after being chased off by cops, Cece still wants to go at it. Even after sending her all around Lagos, she still thought I was fool enough to believe her bullshit story. How I wanted to be a fly on the wall at that UPS office! The situation was getting ridiculous; it was time I pulled the rug.

From: Kelly B
To: Miss Cece Browne <Ccbebe66@yahoo.com>
Date: July 12, 2004 1:45 p.m.

Re: Laptop for Sale

Dear Cece or whoever the fuck you are,

You are a liar and a thief. I hope you had fun running around Lagos looking for your money. I sure did! Just in case you haven't figured it out, there is NO MONEY, OK?! Next time you want to swindle someone out $1,100, you should remember not all of us are idiots. You fucked with the wrong person my friend.

God Bless,

Kelly (a.k.a Allie Baba—you fucker!!!!)

REPLY to: k7p4h-9852130076@comm.cl.org

posted: 2005-10-30 1:43 am EDT

Lost Mojo. Need help finding it!

I have lost my mojo somewhere within the five boroughs and I desperately need it back. It's full of spunk, always knows the right thing to say, and is deceptively charming. It likes to socialize (sometimes a little too much!) and is comfortable meeting new people—can make friends with a stump. When separated from its owner for too long, it may become hostile. Was last seen on the corner of Orchard St and Rivington.

If you've seen it around or are keeping it in your back pocket, please return it back to me. No questions asked, I promise. I'm afraid the longer my mojo and I are separated, more bad dates will incur.

- Location: New York
- It's NOT okay to solicit this person with services or other unrelated interests

Lost

It was the weekend and I was meeting some friends at our frequent watering hole, No Malice Palace—a dive bar so deep on Avenue B, if you blinked, you'd miss the lonely bouncer out front. The weather had just turned crisp and the bar's red walls coupled with a nice drink were warm enough to take the chill off the loneliest of hearts, including mine.

Since I was the first to arrive, I parked myself on a cracked vinyl stool and ordered a beer from the young stud behind the bar. There was nothing better than the sight of a tight set of buns to keep a girl occupied while she waited. No Malice Palace was a place known for stocking their bar with as many sizzling bartenders as top shelf liquors—most of them recent transplants who served up drinks with a dash of Midwestern charm and rugged good looks. It was this perfect formula that kept the bar packed with ladies night after night, competing for a chance to get into a pair of coveted undies.

Even if you weren't lucky enough to snag a bartender's digits by the end of the night, No Malice Palace was still a magnet for adventure if you were single and out for some fun. Every dark corner and barstool held an opportunity to collide with someone.

Tonight, as I minded my own business, I was rear-ended by a tall man with a spare Michelin tire wrapped around his belly.

"Bartender, Wild Turkey on the rocks. Thank ya my good sir." His voice had a strong southern twang.

He tossed a twenty dollar bill on the counter, and sat down at an empty barstool positioned a little too close to mine. I flashed him a courtesy smile and noticed there was more to this guy than his flourished accent. Atop his head was a ten gallon hat and slung around his neck was a thick gold chain that reached to his bellybutton. Swinging at the chain's base, like a bedazzled pendulum, was a chocolate frosted doughnut covered in rainbow sprinkles.

"Well, howdy there, little lady," he said with a tip of his hat.

Was this some kind of joke? My eyes scoured the place for hidden cameras but couldn't find any.

"Howdy yourself. Enjoying your time in New York?" I asked.

"That obvious? What gave it away—the hat?"

"More like that necklace. It's quite spectacular."

"Ah, this beauty—she's a real looker, alright. Wouldn't leave the house without her." He slipped the chain between his fingers and rubbed the metal as if it was a delicate piece of meat.

The bartender set down his whiskey and threw me a muffled smirk like I had just opened the floodgates to Crazytown.

"I've never seen a gold chain so long before," I asked. "Is it real?"

My new friend's expression turned from interest to indignation in an instant. "Best watch those manners, missy. People should be on a first name basis before they go around asking what's real and what's not. Are those dangly things you call earrings real or plastic?"

"I didn't mean to offend," I stammered. "I'm just dazzled by your choice of jewelry. It takes a whole lotta man to pull off that kind of necklace. I'm Kelly, by the way."

I offered out my hand and he shook it.

"Name's Bill." He puffed up his chest and set back his drink. "And to answer your question—yes, it's fourteen karats. But don't go on telling everyone it is real 'cause I ain't looking to get mugged tonight."

"Oh, I would never do that." I drew a zipper across my lips. "Your secret's safe with me."

His eyes caught my ring-less left hand and a smile escape his lips. "So Kelly, tell me why a pretty gal like you is sitting at a bar all alone?"

"Oh, I'm not really alone. I'm meeting some people here in a few minutes. Look, I gotta ask because it's like the big rhino in the room: What is the deal with the doughnut?"

His eyebrows raised a wee bit. "You're attracted to it aren't ya? No need to be shy..."

"Ummm, I'm not sure attracted is the right word. Curious is more like it. I guess it all depends if you'd let me take a bite out of it."

It was bad enough I engaged the man in conversation, but now I was soliciting a tasting off his belly?! My desire for the doughnut had overwritten every logical fiber of my being. I wanted to touch it, eat it, feel its warm sugary goodness roll over my desperate taste buds. Oh god, how I wished I hadn't skipped dinner. Bill slapped back my eager fingers before they entered his personal space.

"Now you hold on just one minute, missy! You don't go around touching other people's doughnuts. It's not right." He coddled the pastry as if it were a baby in his womb.

"Oh come on, please," I begged, "I have to know—is it real or plastic?"

"Why?"

"Is your real name Homer Simpson?"

"Who the hell is Homer? Looky here, all I wanted to do was have a nice drink. What are you, the pap-par-razzieee asking me all these personal questions? I never said I wanted to do an exposé."

I was making him flustered. He looked around as if he wanted to get away. He wasn't going anywhere, not until I found out the truth.

"You sure you're not a part of some reality show? Are there hidden cameras planted around here I can't see?"

"Sorry, ma'am. I don't know anything about no reality show."

"What will it take for you to let me handle your doughnut? I've got a dingdong in my purse. You show me yours and I'll show you mine." I winked.

"Now you're just pulling my chain."

"Do you hear that?" I bent an ear towards my stomach. "Your pastry is driving my stomach crazy. Chocolate frosted doughnuts are my favorite. Ever switch them up? Say, with a French cruller?"

He nodded with the tip of his cowboy hat. "I've been known to dabble in a cruller now and then."

"And the jelly doughnut?"

"Now the jelly can get plain messy."

"So, come on. What do you say? You gonna let me have a nibble or what? Or are you going to leave a girl starving?"

There was no response.

"Pretty please?" I pleaded. "I promise not to eat the whole thing. Just a wee nibble. Surely you can spare a sprinkle or two."

"Let me think about that for a moment..."

He finished the last of his drink, wrapped his hands around the back of his neck, and concentrated hard on the request. In the meantime, I looked around and noticed the bar was filling up fast with after-work heels and sneakered locals. The chatter had gotten louder and so had the mood, as a deejay cranked hip hop beats from the back of his booth.

Suddenly, reality took hold and a pang of fear washed over me. My friends were supposed to be here any moment. What if they caught me eating Bill's doughnut? I guess I could blame it on the cold medication I had taken. All I knew was my taste buds were on a dangerous mission. If I hadn't lost my mojo, none of this would be happening.

After two tortuous minutes Bill had finally caved in and gave me the green light. "Alright, go on now. Take a bite."

"For a second there I thought I lost you in meditation. I can't believe you're agreeing to this."

"Well, you asked a very serious thing of me. Not just anyone gets to sample my sweets. But only a little taste. Any more, and you're going to buy me a new one." He laid out the law with a firm finger.

Somewhere in the back of my mind, a voice was screaming: *What the hell are you doing? Who knows where that doughnut has been!* But it was too late, my hands were already lifting the frosted pastry off his belly; the chocolate frosting felt warm to the touch. I adjusted the golden tether and took a nice sized bite, leaving behind a full set of dental imprints.

"I said only one bite," he said, yanking back his necklace. "Your mouth is like a bear trap!"

In the background a familiar female voice said, "Uh, Kelly? What are you doing?"

Blood rushed to my face. I turned around and behind me stood my oldest friend, Bea; standing next to her was her boyfriend, Alex, and his friend.

"Heeey," I said, painfully aware of the sprinkle stuck to my cheek. I tried to discreetly tuck it into the corner of my mouth, but it rolled off my cheek and landed on my sweater like a colored marker for my nipple. *So much for playing it cool,* I thought. "So," I said with a nervous laugh, "you guys just get here?"

"About a minute ago. You're looking settled. Want to introduce me to your new friend?" Bea's steely gray eyes scanned Bill from head to toe as he mended the mess I made of his twisted chain. I shook my head no, feeling guilty.

"Well then, let me introduce you to Alex's friend, Louis. He just moved here from Paris. Come on and let's go find someplace to sit in the back." She leaned over and she plucked the sprinkle off my chest. "I think you dropped this."

I swiped it from her outstretched finger and swallowed it before anyone else spotted the evidence. The three of them went off in search of a couch while I sorted out my tab and the rest of my loose rainbow-colored thread.

"I never would've figured you as an eat-and -run kinda gal," said Bill. "Maybe I shouldn't have letcha move in so fast." He leaned over the bar and ordered another glass of whiskey.

I stared at the teeth marks around the doughnuts edge and cringed. "We did move a little fast, didn't we?"

"So who's the lucky fella?" He thumbed to the back of the bar.

"Some guy from Paris. My friend wants to set us up."

"I hear those Parisians make good pastries—all those crescents and such."

"But none will be as tasty as yours, Bill."

"Now, no need to drag this out. You got a fancy French cruller to bite. Better hope he's worth it."

I left Bill at the bar, not sure what to make of his fate. A few hours later, I realized his prognosis was not good. As the night progressed, time and the whiskey hadn't been kind to him. The doughnut, which once worked as a conversation piece, was now a repellant, scaring all women within a two-foot radius. I was relieved not to be on that barstool; instead I was snuggled up on a couch, listening to the sexy voice of my new Parisian friend, Louis.

"You like salmon, oui?" he asked, sliding in closer to me.

From the bar some girl shouted out, *'Ewh, get that thing away from me, creep.'* I instinctively knew to peek in Bill's direction. "I'm sorry, what was that? I couldn't hear you over all the shouting."

"I was speaking of fish, but I zee your eyes are on that man with zee doughnut."

"Oh, him," I winced. "I feel kinda bad for him."

"Why is zis? Because you ate his pastry?"

My face flushed redder than an angry pimple. "Oh my God, you weren't supposed to see that. I don't know what I was thinking."

"Actually, when I saw zis, I thought I need to know zis woman."

"Really?"

Louis leaned in close and explained his reasoning. "A man like zis will never get attention without, how do you say in English—*accoutrements*. You were kind to talk to him when most women would turn away. Zis tells me you are not only sexy, but are a good person. It makes me want to know more about you. So, tomorrow—we meet at my house for dinner, yes?"

"Whatever you make, do me a favor and don't wear it around your neck. I don't want to bite off more than I can chew."

He flashed a coy smile. "Never. I only do zis with my desserts."

"Well then, I'll make sure to bring my appetite."

posted: 2005-10-31 3:58 pm EDT

Found Beer Goggles

I found these perfectly good beer goggles in my purse. They must have slipped into my bag while out with friends. If you were anywhere near the vicinity of Avenue B and 3rd Street last night, there is a good chance these are yours.

I read that too much exposure to beer goggles can result in unwanted and questionable behavior. Considering their warning label, I would love to get these back to their rightful owner ASAP. You have until tomorrow to claim them before they end up in the trash. Serious inquiries only!!!

● Location: New York
● It's NOT okay to solicit this person with services or other unrelated interests

Found

It was official. Despite my shenanigans, I had landed my first proper date in over a year. This was great news, except there was one slight problem—I couldn't remember much beyond my doughnut-munching escapade. The cold meds I was on hadn't mixed well with my drinks and I got a wee bit boozier than I thought. In fact, if it hadn't been for Louis's message, I wouldn't have known I was going to his place for dinner.

On the walk over to his apartment I attempted to jog my memory. As much as I tried, the picture was so hazy I could barely envision a face. Sights and sounds came in as flashes on a corrupted memory card: Red couch, a slurry of French words, dim candles, pounding bass, ditzy dancers, crushed feet, Louis's sweaty palm, me jotting my number down with a leaky pen.

When Louis answered the door in an apron and purple stained lips, standing a foot too short, I blinked my eyes a couple of times. This was the man I spent last night snuggling with? His wet eyes were spread too far apart. He was more like a frog than I ever imagined. Damn beer goggles and their tainted lenses. There should be some kind of warning against wearing eye gear four inches too thick.

"*Bon soir*," said Louis, his bloodshot eyes comfortably at half-mast. Wafting out the door was a carpet of gray clouds. It was the skunky smoke of a lit blunt. "Beinvenue to my home. Entre, entrez-vous."

I bent down and we exchanged a kiss on each cheek. He slipped his arm inside mine and led me into his humble abode. Looking positively Parisian, I pulled a baguette from my purse and handed it to him.

"I'm not sure how it will compare to the ones you're used to, but I made a special trip to Balthazar. They're said to make the best baguettes this side of the Seine. I thought you might appreciate a little slice of home. It's the least I could do after you slaved away in the kitchen," I said, taking note of his chef's gear.

"Slave? No, not so much." He wagged his finger. "Don't let the apron fool you. I am no chef, only a poor cook. Come, let me take your things and pour you a drink."

Louis took my coat and purse and led me over to the living area. In the center of the blue painted room was a low-slung couch and a glass coffee table. Off to one side was an open kitchen and a candle-lit laminate dining-room table set for two. Apart from the initial smell of pot smoke and cigarettes, his place was cleaner than expected.

I settled into the couch and Louis brought over an open bottle of wine. He poured me a hefty glass and refilled his to the brim. *Mental note: take it easy tonight; the last thing you want is a repeat of last night's performance.*

"Zee rice will be done in a minute," he said, checking the time on his Rolex. "While I finish dinner, perhaps you would like a smoke? Please, relax and make yourself comfortable. I have some salmon that needs attending."

He plucked the half lit blunt from a Waterford crystal ashtray, took a big puff and offered it to me.

"Pourquoi no?" I said, and pinched the blunt from his fingers.

I took a toke and silently laughed at my rudimentary French. Twelve years of studying the language and a father who spoke it fluently, and "pourquoi" was the extent of my vocabulary.

Louis walked over to a small stereo player and popped in a CD of Serge Gainsbourg. He described the French pop singer as "one of zee best musicians in the world, even better than that big-lipped Mick Jagger."

Over Serge's sultry voice, I sipped my vino and watched Louis man the kitchen. In between the guttural grumblings, he sliced my baguette and prepped the plates. A man who knew his way around a kitchen was such a sexy thing...if only he came in a taller, slightly less reptilian-looking package.

A few minutes later he set the plates down and beckoned me over. "Voilà, mon cheri. C'est fini. As you Americans say: Dinner is served. Bon appetit."

"Perfect timing, I'm starving. I can't wait to see what you whipped up."

My munchie-filled brain had been so caught up in French landscapes of poached salmon and tangy hollandaise sauces, I didn't realized the effects of Louis's weed were a bit stronger than expected. When I reached the table my hunger was at a fevered pitch. I dove into my seat, excited and anxious to eat. But all it took was one glance at the plate for my heart and appetite to shatter into a million pieces. Instead of being presented with a culinary masterpiece, what I found—staring up at me like the sad eyes of an orphaned child—were two heaping balls of waterlogged rice and a soggy pile of overcooked string beans.

Across the table, Louis was ripping open a plastic package of smoked salmon with his teeth. The orange price tag indicated it was on sale—*sacre bleu!*—for a whopping dollar and ninety-nine cents. Good lord. I flinched when I saw the expiration date was two days past.

My mother's words rang around my head: *Don't be rude, Kelly. Remember all those starving children in Africa who would trade their lives for the food on your plate.* She was right, food was food and I was hungry as a wildebeest. At that moment I would have eaten a stale Eucharist if it was offered.

In between bites of the cold, stringy salmon, my mind drifted back to that Frenchman in the kitchen. Louis had looked so official in his apron. All he needed was a little hat and I would've thought he was a graduate of the Cordon Bleu. *So much for enjoying some authentic Parisian fare,* I thought. His skills in the kitchen were as useless as my French. Had I known, I would've brought over a bag of mini-bagels and cream cheese and spared him the effort.

If it wasn't for Serge's singing and the occasional comment, our meal was eaten in awkward silence. Thank God I wasn't the only one who thought the dinner was less than a success. Louis and I managed to avoid much eye contact with the limp food on our forks by shooting half smiles and furtive glances towards the ceiling. When the silence became a little too deafening, Louis popped open another bottle of vino and poured another round of drinks, significant in proportion. So much for my drink limit.

When the remains of our uninspired meal were scraped into the trashcan, Louis and I were properly buzzed and, like last night, back on the couch debating the finer points of life. Tonight's topic of conversation was our hometowns.

"How can you say New York is original when even your Lady of Liberty was a gift from zee French?"

"All I'm trying to say is, New York has just as much character as Paris. What, do you think the French are the only ones who know how to make a beautiful building? Look at the Chrysler Building. It's as iconic as the Eiffel Tower, for Christ's sake. "

"Pah, next you are going to tell me that *ug-lee* black box you call zee Seagram Building is pretty. You Americans can have such *tack-ee* style. Spend some time with me in Paris, we will walk the streets of my birth on Île St. Louis. Then you will know the meaning of beauty. You see this neighborhood I live in now, and most of New York is so *ug-lee*. I don't know how you people can love such a filthy city."

Now I loved Paris as much as the next person, but sitting there watching Louis's flat lips babble on about how much he hated my town made me wonder why I was still there. I could be home right now in my sweatpants, my head buried in a bin of ice cream. Shit, *The Apprentice* was almost on! From where I was sitting, Donald Trump's hair had more appeal than Louis.

I was ready to wrap things up and save dessert for my couch, when something happened. Louis put his hand on top of mine. That small touch changed everything.

A shot of excitement surged through my skin; it made the hairs on my arms twinge. A man's touch, oh it had been so long since I remembered it. Delight soon turned into hate as I chided myself for being so pathetic and lonely.

Louis was a cheap, overindulgent snob—three things I detested. How much was I going to forgive for a night of heavy petting? Last night I allowed my mouth dangerously close to a stranger's belly button, all for a chocolate-frosted nibble. From that repulsive perspective, I had come a long way in the last twenty-four hours. By last night's standards, this was a step up in the world. Louis was a catch, the closest thing to a real winner.

He saddled up close. The tips of his salmon-greased fingers grazed my cheek.

"You look like your mind is somewhere else. Why don't you come here and give me a kiss?"

Now I could list all the reasons why this scenario was wrong, but in the end I did what he asked and kissed him.

His fat, fishy tongue rolled around my mouth in a series of figure eights. He tasted like a wine cork soaked too long in an ashtray. I closed my eyes, plugged my nose and let my mind drift to distant shores—a place far away, filled with bronzed Greek gods and sparkling seas. His roaming hands pinched my skin. They grappled over my shoulders and thighs. My body was his Mount Everest: a peak he was determined to climb.

He hoisted me into his arms and began walking down the hallway. I felt like a gigantic squid compared to his small size. My long limbs tried and failed to slither away from his tight grip.

"Where are you taking me?" I asked. His bedroom was in sight.

"What do you mean where am I taking you. Why the bedroom, of course."

"I'm no slut, in case you didn't know."

He heaved my elongated body onto the bed. "I thought we'd be more comfortable here, no?"

I looked around at his boudoir of love, the place where he made magic happen. A few pictures of his family and friends from back home were tacked on the wall above a small writing desk. Several photos looked as if a person had been strategically cut off of the edges. The pillowcases were covered with tiny yellow flowers. He closed my eyes and kissed me again. The springs squeaked beneath the flimsy mattress.

"You are so sexy," his hot voiced growled in my ear. "I just want to eat you all over."

He pounced on me. His exploring hands reached under my shirt and tickled my skin. I felt him grow hard beneath his jeans.

Don't do this Kelly. You're not even attracted to him. Are you really this lonely? This is all wrong. You'll regret it tomorrow...

He pressed his proud bulge against my leg. His hand grabbed hold of my mouth and he kissed me again. I imagined this is what it must be like to eat a hot tongue sandwich. *For Christ's sake!* my mind screamed. He was French. Weren't they experts in the fine art of kissing? How come no one taught this man to make out? This was a disaster.

"Oh God," his voiced purred over and over, like a stalled motor.

I needed air. His moaning and groaning was too overwhelming. There was only one thing to do. I had to turn the tables. It was time to lighten up the mood and to show off my wrestling moves. I shoved him off with my foot in his chest.

"You are such a sexy animal," he laughed as he flew across the bed.

"Sexy, you say? Just wait and you'll see."

I flipped him around and rammed his face in the pillow. My legs clamped around his waist and I used his butt as a seat. With a big heave I yanked his legs and lumbar up towards me. It was a pleasure watching his body torque into a C.

"Ohlalalalalahahahahahaha," he squealed. "I give up! Let me go!"

A few minutes of panting and begging and I finally released the hold. That should have done it. I hoped Louis's passions would've settled. Oh, how wrong was that thought. He sprang at me with more vigor and pinned my arms to the bed.

"I love a woman who knows her way around *zee boudoir*. I want to do something to you. I promise you will like. Will you let me do it to you? Yes? I promise I won't bite."

I brushed the hair away from my sweaty forehead and took a moment to catch my breath. "Depends on what you want to do. You have to tell me first."

"Oh no, I can't say, I can only do."

His hips shimmied side to side. His tongue flickered across his purple lips like a snake.

I knew where he was going with this. What was there left to do? Another Boston Crab or a purple nurple wasn't going to be enough of a deterrent. I had to think fast. It was time to get dirty. What was the one thing sure to be a man repellant?

"Look, I know where this is headed and I have to say no. I swear it has nothing to do with you. It's just that I've got my *period*."

Never in my life had I witnessed a man fling himself so quickly from a woman than Louis did in that instant. To top it off, he swiped a hand across his head like he had just dodged a bullet.

"Oh, thank god," he shouted. "Thank God, thank God, THANK GOD!"

"Geez, it isn't that big of a deal. Women get it every month."

"Let me ask you a question: Do you get bad PMS?"

Did I hear that right? "PMS? No, not really. Why?"

"A-plus-plus in my book! When my ex-girlfriend got her period, she used to throw cans of tuna at my head!"

"Did she ever hit you with one?" I found myself sympathizing and hoped that she did.

"Oui! You see ziss mark on my forehead." He pointed to a small dent above his right eye. "Zat is from one of her cans. She nearly made me blind!" He pretended to spit, and shouted out, "What a *putain!*"

This was my cue; the perfect moment to put an end to this night. I rolled off the bed and unruffled my clothing.

"Look, it's getting kind of late. I should get going."

He looked shocked. "So soon? It is not because of what I said of my ex-girlfriend?"

"No, no. I've got work early tomorrow," I lied. *Your ex-girlfriend is the least of your problems, buddy...*

"Are you sure you don't want to smoke another—"

"If I don't leave now I'll never get up in the morning."

The words followed me down the hall and into the living room.

A moment later, Louis was at the foot of the hallway. His disappointed face watched me collect my things.

"But you can't go. Not now." He glanced towards the bathroom. "You see, I even cleaned my shower."

"Cleaned your shower?" Now I was really confused.

"Mais oui! I thought you'd want to shower in a clean place. You know... *for afterwards.*"

Huh? It took me a moment to process what he had just said. I tossed on my jacket and purse and opened the front door.

"Wow, how presumptuous. For a French guy you know *nothing* about women. It's a pity I don't have a can of tuna handy. I see a spot on your forehead that could use another good whacking."

For the next two weeks Louis's desperate phone calls were shoved straight into voice mail. In the end, the only thing he kept asking was, "What did I do? Was it something I said?"

posted: 2006-03-19 10:11 am EDT

NEED WOOD. BUILDING NOAH'S ARK

I'm embarking on a mission to build Noah's Ark according to God's instructions and need help. As per his specs in Genesis, the ark will be 473ft long by 95 ft across and 45ft high. At the moment, I have about a third of the wood but need the generosity of others to get the project sailing. Once the ark is built, I will begin the arduous task of collecting the animals.

If there is a kind soul out there willing to unload planks of wood, please contact me and we can arrange a pick-up or drop off. The sooner the better. I'd like to complete the ark before hurricane season starts.

Godspeed.

- Location: Bronx
- It's NOT okay to solicit this person with services or other unrelated interests

---

From: Fred Kaplan <Fredkapster@aol.com>
To: ptoqr-76739247095@sales.cl.org
Date: June 14, 2006 1:26 p.m.

Subject: Need Wood, Building Noah's Ark

Hi there,

I've got a boatload of wood sitting around in my backyard. If you don't mind the smell of raccoon piss, it's all yours.

Freddie

From: Kelly B <kellyb@hotmail.com>
To: Fred Kaplan <Fredkapster@aol.com>
Date: June 14, 2006 3:34p.m.

Re: Need Wood, Building Noah's Ark

Good afternoon Freddie,

While you're offer is tempting, I'm afraid the scent of raccoon urine might pose a problem later on when I get the animals on board. Thanks anyway.

Onward and upward!
K

From: **T-rex 976**<T-rex976@earthlink.com>
To: ptoqr-76739247095@sales.cl.org
Date: June 14, 2006 6:01 p.m.

Subject: Need Wood, Building Noah's Ark

Hey Noah,
I got wood for you. It's a log, 7 inches long and solid like a rock. You can come down and lick it up anytime you like. Pics available if you want.

T-rex

From: **Kelly B** <kellyb@hotmail.com>
To: T-rex976<T-rex976@earthlink.com>
Date: June 14, 2006 8:12 p.m.

Re: Need Wood, Building Noah's Ark

Dear T-Rex,

Unless it's hard like mahogany and can withstand a lot of hammering, I don't think your wood will be a good fit.

Thanks anyway.
K

From: T-rex976
To: Kelly B <kellyb@hotmail.com>
Date: June 14, 2006 11:38 p.m.

Re: Need Wood, Building Noah's Ark

My log is 8" of black Gaboon ebony. It's hard as hell and used to a TON of hammering.

T-rex

From: Kelly B
To: T-rex976 <T-rex976@earthlink.com>
Date: June 15, 2006 2:22 p.m.

Re: Need Wood, Building Noah's Ark

Dear T-rex,

Sorry to have misled you. According to the specs in Genesis, the plans prefer a lighter wood than ebony. If your log was from Cypress then I would gladly go down and take it off your hands.

Perhaps your ebony will come in handy on another project. In the future I would like to make a clarinet. For now, I will continue my search elsewhere. Thanks for the interest.

Godspeed,
K

From: T-rex976
To: Kelly B <kellyb@hotmail.com>
Date: June 15, 2006 5:13 p.m.

Re: Need Wood, Building Noah's Ark

Whenever you want, you can play with my wood any day.

T-rex

From: Jane G <JaneG@petapets.org>
To: ptoqr-76739247095@sales.cl.org
Date: June 19, 2006 11:13 a.m.

Subject: Need Wood, Building Noah's Ark

Good morning,

My name is Jane Goodault and I work with *PetaPets*, a non-for-profit organization which ensures the safety of animals from neglect and abuse. Your advertisement on Craigs.org was flagged by a member of our staff due to the nature of its content. As the largest welfare representative of the animal kingdom, we have a number of concerns regarding your upcoming project.

In such cases where animals are to be boarded and shipped out to sea, *PetaPets* has a moral duty to ensure that all the animals on your ark will be handled properly, treated humanely, and ethically sourced.

Regarding our safety concerns, could you please address some of the specifics of the ark such as: stable heights and width, sewage treatment facilities, how you intend to handle such a wide variety of species in close proximity, and whether you would be following international zoological crating guidelines?

This is in no way a comprehensive list of questions. If you would like some guidance on the nature of animal oceanic travel or more, we at *PetaPets* are willing to help you in this process.

"All of God's creatures, big and small, deserve a good life..." –Ansel Marks, founder and president of PetaPets Organization.

We look forward to hearing from you.
Have a good day.
Sincerely,
Jane Goodault
Watchdog Operational Manager

From: **Kelly B** <kellyb@hotmail.com>
To: JaneG <JaneG@petapets.org>
Date: June 19, 2006 12:05 p.m.

Re: Need Wood, Building Noah's Ark

Dear Jane,

I appreciate PetaPets' interest in my ark. Rest assured all necessary precautions will be applied to ensure the safety of the animals. It is my vow that no animal shall be mistreated or harmed while in my care. As for any specificities of the project, may I recommend you to Genesis Chapters 6-9 of the Bible for a more accurate description of God's intentions.

As the project moves forward, I will be requiring the services of several zoological consultants, in addition to the two full-time veterinarian doctors I have hired to be on board once we set sail. Both doctors are to be board certified in both mammals and exotic animals, and are skilled in animal dentistry. If you have any recommendations for qualified zoological consultants, I would welcome the help when the time comes.

I hope you and the PetaPets organization will find the information I provided gives some peace of mind. It is my mission to serve and protect as God's will.

My best regards,
Kelly

From: Law offices of Fanranny, Lanfoot & Rye
To: ptoqr-76739247095@sales.cl.org
Date: June 20, 2006 11:13 a.m.

Subject: Need Wood, Building Noah's Ark

To whom it may concern:

This is a cease and desist letter from the law offices of Fanranny, Lanfoot & Rye. Our client—Evangelist Pastor Noah Brown of *Noah's Ark Commissions ltd.*—lays claims of infringement on the trademark Noah's Ark Commissions. Pastor Noah Brown is the owner of several trademarks, including but not limited to, the below mentioned United States Trademark Registrations:

Noah's Ark Commissions ltd.—131445672—4/5/2002
Noah's Ark Consortium llc.—156112903—6/2/2002
Noah's Ark Funpark and Wildrides—209937261—12/10/2004

Of which, these trademarks are identified as Classes 8 and 10 and are used in connection with the manufacturing and distributing of Noah's Ark replicas, Noah's Ark structures, Noah's Ark wooden toys and any other biblical Noah ark references for the purpose of making a profit. These registrations constitute conclusive evidence of Pastor Noah Brown's ownership of Noah's Ark, as well as his exclusive use of these rights.

It has come to our attention that your advertisement on Craigs.org is an infringement upon our client's intellectual property rights. The infringing material can be found on Craigs.org ID number 76739247095, posted on March 19, 2006, 10:11 am.

Accordingly, Mr. Noah Brown requests you cease your online marketing campaign bearing the name Noah's Ark and relinquish the advertisement henceforth. Mr. Noah Brown has a good faith belief that the above identified advertisement is not authorized by Mr. Brown, his agents or the law.

This request is made without waiver of any of Mr. Brown's rights or remedies, all of which are expressly reserved.

I declare under penalty of perjury that the foregoing is true and correct and that I am authorized to act on behalf of Mr. Brown et al.

Regards,
Montague Fanranny III Esq.

Dear Craig,

It has recently come to my attention there is a severe deficit of intelligence within the general populace. Unfortunately, I'm sorry to say many of these bozos use your services like their lives depended on it. I can attest to this sad fact after I received a cease-and-desist letter for an ad I placed on your site. A lawyer named Montague Fanranny the third (*I swear that is his real name*) is forcing me to shut down an ad I placed looking for scraps of wood to help build Noah's Ark. Apparently, some guy named Noah already has dibs on the world of ark building. I realize I violated your Terms of Use and for that I am truly sorry. I admit I had no intention of building an ark, nor did I really *need* any wood. I was just bored as fuck. Any chance you'll forgive my momentary lapse into dumbsidedness?

Speaking of idiots, myself included, have you noticed how this whole World Wide Web has turned into a carnival of freaks? It's only been, what—a whole ten years or so since people began signing onto the Internet? What the hell happened to society in this last decade? At the flick of an electronic switch, the human race turned into a bunch of babbling baboons and the Internet our pulpit. Google was just declared a verb. God help us. When did the whole planet get flipped on its head?

It feels like it was only last week when I bought my first modem: a 56k dial-up. Do you remember it? The damn thing was a modern revelation back then. The day I set sail on my maiden voyage into the Ethernet, I was navigating with a fifty-pound Toshiba Satellite—the world's first color laptop. Using a rusty compass and a sundial as my guide, I surfed my way to Wu Tang Clan's 36 chambers before settling on the sands of Saint Tropez on rumors that several black-and-white pics of a naked Brad Pitt had washed up on shore. The load of his supersized pixels almost sunk my Satellite, and it took hours before I caught a glimmer of skin. Too bad the only thing visible in the checkered mess was the man's damn pinky toe. Oh, but what a darling piece of phalange it was! Boy, those were the days of You've Got Mail, chat rooms and real MEGA pixels. Now each time I enter this cyber vortex, life seems cluttered. People are meaner, the chatter dumber, folks more perverted. Case in point, the responses from my ark ad were either sex fiends, animal fanatics, or litigious lawyers. The more connected the world is, the more we've become separated.

So much for technology, I'm ready to ditch the digital and go analog. Fuck computers and cell phones. It's time to brush the dust off the old oil lamps and rotary phones! Laugh if you want, but wait and see what happens when that technological apocalypse comes. All I've got to say is thank God for my solar-powered calculator. Do you know how to do a square root without one? I'm banking on that little gizmo being the human race's savior—if or when the time comes. Archaeologists are still scratching their sunburned heads over how the Greeks built the Parthenon without one.

Despite all this talk of ancient wonders and their modern day rivals, there really is something to be said for simplicity. Watch, the next time we chat I'll be churning my own butter! But don't expect me to don a bonnet. A girl has to draw a line in the sand of time somewhere. These days, mine falls somewhere between 1898 and 1929.

So hey, I realized I never did properly thank you for setting me up with that wannabe Keanu Reeves lookalike a few years back. Life occupied both of us and for one reason or another, I forgot or was trying my best to erase it from my memory since it was such an epic disaster. And yet, I'm frustrated to say, all these years later, I'm still out in the field hoping to score my fly ball. I got to thinking (yeah I know, it's bad for my health) you've been in New York for a while. You have probably amassed quite a collection of friends in all this time. Maybe one of them might be looking for a nice dinner date? I swear I won't resort to gypsy parlor tricks unless it is absolutely necessary! If you're up to playing cupid again, I'll help sharpen your arrows.

And once again, I'm so sorry about the whole Noah's Ark bit. Hopefully once the ad is gone, these crazy lawyers will leave me alone. I promise to make sure your name stays out of this bogus trademark infringement case. In the meantime, I'll keep my eyes out for any prospects you send my way. I've got my fingers crossed!

Thanks again Craig. You're the best!

posted: 2006-07-01 10:43 am EDT

7/28 - THIS FRIDAY NIGHT 1920's SWING DANCE NYC!!! (Midtown)

Dancers of all levels are welcome to kick up their heels and join the legendary swing band The Fat Cats for a night of fun for everyone. The festivities are held at Swing 46, a supper club with live music, located in the heart of midtown Manhattan at 326 West 46th Street.

Doors open at 9 p.m. Admission $15, includes one signature drink the "City Sidecar". Print coupon for offer.

Zoot suits encouraged, sneakers prohibited, twinkle toes required!

- Location: New York
- It's NOT okay to solicit this person with services or other unrelated interest

Events

It was Friday night and I was in the peppermint-pink colored bedroom of my brainiest friend, Ana. She was a genius, the youngest Einstein born into a family with so much brain capacity their combined IQs could launch a fleet of rocket ships. In college she was that girl who breezed through academia collecting 4.0's each semester. As an adult, her ambitions led her towards a career as a celebrated microbiologist, and as is the case with Nobel Prize contenders, we never got as much time to hang as we wanted.

Ana spent half of the year in Costa Rica studying the reproductive habits of newts. When she wasn't freezing samples of reptilian tails for DNA research, she worked on her dissertation in the apartment where she had grown up—a head of dark curly hair stuffed inside way too many books. But Ana wasn't your typical nerd who only had passions for code sequences and writing computer analysis programs. In between drawing the molecular breakdowns of Twinkies and Cheetos to the amusement of her friends, Ana loved salsa dancing, eating Cuban food, and sweating for hours in 180 degree hot yoga rooms. She lived a double life, and her annual trips down south usually ended the same way. By the time her six months were up in the swampy tropics, listening to a chorus of bullfrogs and fighting mosquitos, Ana was ready to burn off some steam, pining for home and human contact. She made up for the lost time by dragging along reluctant souls like me out for a night of promised fun.

Tonight, she swore, was going to be extra special for me. She and her Nigerian boyfriend Diji had concocted a plan to take their friends out for a night of swing dancing. There was an ulterior motive of course; there was a guy that Diji insisted I meet. His name was Chad, a former child chess player and the son of a famed astrologer.

"Is this a surprise?" I asked. "Or does Diji's friend know that he's getting fixed up?"

Ana was at the mirror, zipping up a poodle skirt.

"Kelly, it's cool. It's all under control. Just a group meeting. That's why we're bringing Pippa along. Five is a nice, odd number. So what do you think of this skirt? Is it twenties enough?"

She puckered her lips as she stared into a full-length mirror. One hand held a mass of curls in a bun, the other rested on her hip. With her lips still pursed, she twisted and turned. This was the fifth outfit she had tried on. The truth was, it didn't matter what she wore. Even wrapped in a burlap sack, her yoga body looked killer.

Compared to her, I felt like a schlump. I was on the verge of getting a visit from Aunty Erma and my protruding pooch reminded me I was retaining water.

"Your outfit looks fine. Don't try on another," I said. "I want to talk about tonight. Is it true Chad does a lot of swing dancing?"

"I think so," she said, painting her lips a light pink. "Why? Is that a problem?"

"Depends on his dance moves and how deep he gets into his costume."

"I wonder what Diji is wearing? Oh my God, I can't even imagine." She opened a drawer and pulled out a camera. "Put this in your purse. We need to document this event."

"Speak for yourself! You think I want to relive my two left feet out on the dance floor? Are you insane?"

"Enough whining already. You're looking deflated and the night hasn't even begun! You always get this way before your period. Who knows, maybe after tonight you'll quit complaining no one is out there for you. Kelly, you have to open your mind to new experiences."

She was right. It was time I opened my horizons. I sucked it up and tried to look good, despite the ill-fitting clothes.

Our meeting spot was Swing 46, a discreet dance club tucked onto 46th street, steps away from the bright lights of the Times Square district. Swing 46 wore its hat from a bygone era. Its tattered red awning and marquee lights a remnant of a red light district past, where bellbottomed pimps hustled broken hearts and hookers talked smack under corner lampposts. Ten years ago, corporate invasion and a tough-cop mayor changed the whole district. Nowadays, the sanitized version of Times Square has all the glamour and charm of a Sizzler Steakhouse.

Ana and I were the first ones to arrive on the scene, followed shortly by Pippa, who I spotted halfway down the block. She was fussing with the waistband of her skirt and occasionally she'd stop and yank hard on her pantyhose like it was choking her knees. Secretly, I was relieved she looked even more uncomfortable than me.

Underneath the awning she greeted us by saying, "Remind me not to spend money on cheap control-top panty hose again. The whole waistband thingy won't stop rolling down. It's giving me a muffin top and making me look fatter than I already am. Ugh, see what I mean?" She dug her hand inside her skirt and tugged the pantyhose band up past her squashed belly button.

"Welcome to the club. I feel like a bloated whale in this outfit." I said, before being distracted by a taxi. "Whoa, would you take a look at that guy getting out the cab!"

"Oh my god! Chad is that you?" Ana squealed.

Like one of those old movies that pans up from the shoes, little bits of Chad's attire came sharply in view. A pair of black patent leather shoes covered with white spats stepped out of the car, followed by a pinstriped zoot suit, and a hunter green fedora complete with a feather attached.

Ana ran over, ecstatic to greet them.

Pippa giggled and gave me a nudge. "Ha! *Someone* is in store for an interesting evening. He's kind of weird looking. Didn't you say he was some kind of whiz kid?"

" 'Child prodigy' is the term Diji used to describe him. His real-life character was made into that famous chess movie."

"Bobby Fischer? He looks more like Roger Rabbit with that get up. At least he's smart—that's a big plus. Imagine if he becomes your next boyfriend! Oh man, think you'll wear matching swing outfits next time you go dancing?"

"Ew, no! Who says there'll be a next time? You just want me to get a boyfriend now that you've got yourself a Belgium boyfriend. Where is Felipe, by the way?"

"Working. Anyway, why are you hounding me? This was Ana's idea."

"She's got Diji. Same difference. People in love always want to share the wealth."

"Or maybe we're tired of your complaining and want you to be happy?"

"Hmm, I'll think about it...Nope, you don't want me happy. Watching me squirm is *waaay* too much fun. Okay, it's time to shut up. Here they come."

Diji settled the taxi tab, and the three of them sauntered over to where Pippa and I stood. Poor Diji, he looked more like a hustler from the seventies than a twenties swing dancer. His silk pants belled out at the bottom, underneath were a pair of white saddle shoes.

"Ladies, ladies, well how diddly-do? Kelly, Pippa—this is my boy Chad. You girls better watch out. He's a master at swing dancing. This man gots the moves."

Chad tucked his head under his hat, his round cheeks slightly flushed. "Don't believe everything Diji says, he's a good liar. No need to worry—I've only taken a class or two."

"Well, that's a relief," I said. "Because none of us knows how to swing dance, so you're the official expert of this left-foot crew."

Chad led the way and we followed behind. A blast of cold hit us as we entered. The doorway had become our portal into a snow globe of time. Benny Goodman blared from the speakers. Gals and gents wore hair pomade and glitter. The place crawled with stained ruby-red lips. The humidity hung heavy with gin and fresh sweat. Set up like stacked dominos, couples saddled up to the bar and skipped away with their drinks.

We took over a big booth with a full view of the bar. Above it, positioned at every few feet, were small black and white TVs hung from the ceiling. Each showcased a Big Brother's view of the dance floor.

Chad slid in next to me and I grappled to make sense of my first impression. Perhaps things would be different if he weren't wearing that zoot suit. He seemed modest, non-threatening, and with Diji he was quite kind. Yet there was something which had me confused. Was he Asian, European, native Uruguayan, all three, none of the above? I couldn't be sure. His slanted blue eyes and dimpled smile offered me no sort of clues.

Over a round of cocktails, Chad and I swapped personal histories; his was by far more impressive than mine. Chess champ by age ten, an Olympic fencer in his teens. By twenty he had a Classics degree from Princeton University. His pedigree was intimidating. How was I going to keep up with all that? My youth was squandered on Madonna albums and bodega-bought wine coolers. Eight weeks each summer spent at Camp Sloane, smuggling in illegal packs of gum and consuming gallons of red bug juice. A purple hair painter in high school; a pothead in college...if this were an entrance exam, my application would be crushed under a mountain of recycled paper.

Despite our different paths, we had a few areas in common. We loved writing screenplays; our parents read us haikus; we believed in Mercury retrogrades and the benefits of acupuncture. We had a mutual penchant for stinky cheeses and even shared a passionate aversion to raw bananas.

We were laughing and having a good time, then guilt set in when I noticed Pippa staring vacantly at the TV screen, looking bored and lonely. She was my diligent fifth wheel, now she was a straggler to our coupling. Chad noticed her too and whispered in my ear, "What would you say if I asked Pippa to dance? You wouldn't mind, would you?"

I said absolutely not, it was a great time to do it. Pippa secretly loved dancing and was ripe for the plucking. Chad cracked his knuckles and shimmied out of the booth.

"Alright, Pippa, time to see those dancing shoes."

She gave a little resistance, and then said, "Oh well, what the hell."

The minute they were out of sight, Ana and Diji slid over and grilled me for information. Their toothy smiles were so wide they reminded me of lottery winners.

"*Sooo*," Ana cooed. "What do you think? You and Chad look like you're getting cozy. Got any plans for a date?"

Diji chimed in, "See Kel, I told you you'd like him. He's a cool dude. I can tell he's totally into you."

I wanted to share my good vibes with them, really I did. But my eyes were too distracted with what was happening on the TV screen above their heads.

Out on the dance floor, people spun and skirts fluttered. Splits and slides were all part of the show. In the corner of the screen, flopping around limp as a rag doll, was Pippa being steered by Chad on a runaway rollercoaster. She looked out of breath, her bun was in tatters.

I turned to Ana and Diji. "Yikes, Chad is a serious dancer. I hope I don't break a leg."

When the song was over Chad and Pippa returned to the booth. He was energized. She looked exhausted. Sweat poured down her temples, tendrils of hair clung to the back of her neck.

"So who's next?" Chad's cool blue eyes split time between Ana and me until he decided. "Come on, Ana, it is your turn."

"No, no, not me. Grab Kelly, she's dying to dance."

"It's okay, I can sit this one out. It's cool Ana, really."

"Ana, it's got to be you. I'm saving the best girl for last." Chad shot me a wink and gulped down the rest of his drink. Next thing we saw was Ana's reluctant feet being dragged to the dance floor. Diji whooped and hollered.

"Oh boy, that guy is intense!" said Pippa dabbing her red face with a wet napkin. "He sure likes spins. He kept twirling me and twirling. In the end, I was so dizzy I swear I couldn't walk straight. He could have spared us the modesty. Diji—your friend needs to come with a professional warning: 'Watch your feet and take off your jewelry.' Looks like I lost an earring." She frowned when she pinched her empty earlobe. "Now, where is this waitress? I need another drink."

While Pippa flagged down a passing server, Diji and I searched the black-and-white screen for Ana.

"Over there, I see her," Diji shouted.

Ana's tiny frame spun in and out of the shot. A collective wince sounded through the room when she lost control of a turn and bashed into a neighboring couple. Just like Pippa only a few minutes earlier, it was painful watching a friend come undone at the seams.

A waitress came over, pen in hand and ready to take orders. I was thankful for the distraction. In my gut I had one of these psychic feelings that something ominous was pending. The sharp pangs of gas that poked at my insides were an internal warning.

"I'm going to pass on the alcohol," I said to the waitress, my voice suddenly unsteady. "Can you get me a big glass of water?"

Pippa pulled a clipping from her purse and handed it over. "I've got my coupon that says the second round is free. I'll take another sidecar."

Diji slapped my back. "Better get ready, Kelly. Looks like you're next."

"I don't know, Diji. I've got a bad feeling about this."

"If you want to get out there and date, you got to be in it to win it. You worry too much, girl. It's just one dance. This isn't a test."

"Oh, really? Look at what one dance did to your lady. She's a complete mess."

Ana arrived at the table with hair so windswept it looked like she had gone for a ride in an open cockpit. I feared a similar fate awaited me.

"Whew, that was exhausting. I'm so glad it is over." She slid into Digi's comfortable arms. "So, when are we going to get you out there, Mister Cool Guy?"

"Maybe in a little bit. Right now I'm having too much fun watching you girls spin."

Chad made a beeline to the bar and asked for some water. I prayed he'd want to take a break and spare me for a few minutes longer.

Ana whispered across the table. "Be careful. That's all I'm saying. It can get hectic out there. I almost sprained my ankle."

Chad came back with a wad full of napkins and a tall glass of water. He stood there soaking the napkin into the water and wiping down his heat-stricken face. With each swipe I could smell the salt lifting off him.

"Alright Kelly, come on let's go." He tugged my unenthusiastic body off the seat.

"Don't you want to take a break? I mean you've been at it for a little bit now? I don't want you to get heat stroke."

"No way. Now is the perfect time. The band is onstage—they're about to start. This is when the dancing really cranks up!"

Pippa, Ana and Digi twinkled their fingers goodbye to my pleading eyes as Chad escorted me away. The last thing I heard before we hit the dance room floor was Ana wishing me good luck.

Chad took my hand and led me onto the parquet floor. Above us tiny red recording lights shone like colored stars. Oh, how I dreaded being on live TV! It was so exposing, like trying to hide your flabby bits while wearing a bikini in the dead of winter.

The band fired up and their brass belted out the sounds of an old World War II big-band number. About ten other couples danced around us. Some were young, some old, all with a level of professional ability. I suppressed my nerves as Chad started us off with a quick two-step.

"Digi told me you used to do ballet," he shouted over the horns. "You should have no problem."

"That was a *looong* time ago. Don't put your faith in all that."

"It means you have rhythm. No worries. I'm confident you'll keep up."

His thumb tapped out the beats against my right palm. He torqued me into a twist and snapped me back quickly. "See that? You're real natural at this."

A natural to *him*—but to me, I wasn't so sure. My feet were fumbling and I kept stepping on his toes. Just when I thought I had things under control, Chad shoved me into a triple spin.

"Watch out," I pleaded. "A couple more of those and I'll throw up."

"No you won't." He spun me around once more and pulled me back so that I fell into his warm, sweaty embrace. "This is what we call the sweetheart move."

"Aha," I let out a nervous laugh. "I see what you mean. But please—"

"Now we're going to do another move that's even more sweet."

The music cranked into high gear, the horns were on all cylinders. I leaned over and screamed, "Seriously Chad, can we slow it down? My stomach doesn't feel so good."

"Sorry, what was that?" He pretended not to hear. "All right, brace yourself: I'm going to set you off on the count of three. One, two, three—*swing!*"

Holy mother of God. The room started to spin. A deep pocket of bile swam up my throat. Quickly, I swallowed it. The contents of my lunch had officially mounted their first attack. Things were happening so fast. Faces merged and blurred. Trumpets wailed. I struggled to see. Chad latched his wet palm against my hand and looped me back for another turn. This time, my balance was off and my skin had turned green.

I searched for an exit. *Water. A bathroom. Please God, not here!*

My pleas went unanswered. It was too late. My stomach unleashed a slurry of vomit across the dance floor.

Couples scattered. Men dove out of the way. Women screamed. And Chad, poor Chad, sat on the floor clutching a swollen knee.

"I think it's broken," he shouted. "What's wrong with you? Why didn't you stop me?" Disgusted, he swiped off a piece of rigatoni that had landed on his leg.

"Chad, oh my God. I am so sorry. Are you okay? Are you hurt?...I think I need water. Yeah, water would be good. I guess it was something I ate."

"Hell yes, it hurts! Look, apologize later. You're babbling about water, when I need a ambulance. Just get me up!"

By now the musicians had stopped playing and a crowd had formed around us. Some were staring, most were laughing. This was humiliating.

I lifted him to his feet as fast as I could. The whole seat of his pants was covered in splatter. I was so mortified, I almost puked again. We rushed out of the room with a hand over my mouth and Chad's arm slung on my shoulder. I prayed to God no one outside the ballroom had caught what just happened.

Once inside the bar there was no room to escape. Duck and hide? Fat chance. The truth was out there: the red twinkling stars had broadcast the whole shebang. My fifteen seconds of fame wasted on a bloopers reel. By the time we hobbled back to the booth, everyone had seen us. Their sorry faces winced and tossed sympathetic frowns in our direction. I slipped away and locked myself in the bathroom. Ana and

Pippa pried me out after Chad and Diji left in the back of an ambulance. When I finally stepped out of the stall, my cheeks were stained with tears and my throat burned with embarrassment.

Chad refused to see me after that night. I tried my best to say sorry through cards and emails. I even sent him a bouquet of flowers and crosswords after his surgery. He told Diji he wasn't interested, claiming that I was unlucky. He said next time he'd take his father's predictions seriously.

Chad and his father were right, I *was* unlucky. It was my fault he limped away that night with a torn ACL and a ruptured knee. I heard he cried when the doctor informed him it would be months before he could dance again. How else could it be? I vowed never to go out swing dancing again. I doubted Chad would blame me.

posted: 2006-07-31 10:43 am EDT

Lake House Rental + Private Dock! (Belchertown, MA)

Get away from it all and stay at our charming Victorian on the picturesque Arcadian lake in the foothills of Massachusetts's Pioneer Valley.

This 1200 sqft house has 2 bedrooms and 2 recently renovated bathrooms. Enjoy private access to the lake from your own dock! Kayaks and rowboat are available at no additional cost. Brought your own boat? There is a public boat launch at Lake Metacomet, a 5 minute drive from the house.

The main floor has open plan with a generous sized living room/dining room and a fully stocked kitchen to meet any chef's needs. On cold nights cuddle up on the couch and make use of the fireplace. The house is equipped with Internet, washer-dryer, dishwasher, TV-DVD, and a stereo.

We invite you to relax, have fun and enjoy your stay. CALL Robin or Mike for rates at (413) 972-5555. Discount given for stays longer than a week.

- It's NOT okay to solicit this person with services or other unrelated interests

Vacation Rentals

A nyone who has spent a whole summer in New York City will tell you it is hellish. That old adage: streets so hot they'll fry an egg? I can tell you it is one-hundred percent true. Yesterday, the nighttime temp hit a steamy ninety-one degrees. I went downstairs with an egg and a thermometer to test out the theory. The concrete sidewalk was so hot, my sunny-side up egg sizzled in less than a minute. Naysayers still think climate change is not a real thing. God help them. The high heat must be liquefying their brains.

August, the hottest month of the year, was almost upon us and New York was suffering with a record-shattering week of one-hundred degree temperatures. The weathermen declared it a heat wave of epic proportions. Nightly news crews covered stories of kids cooling off in a waterfall of open fire hydrants. The mayor made daily announcements telling the elderly to go to cooling stations. A walk down a single block felt as if you'd walked fifty. Electric companies warned of citywide blackouts and urged people to turn off their appliances and conserve power, as if any self-respecting urbanite would do such a thing.

When a town like New York gets this hot, people visibly turn insane. The other day, down in the bowels of the 42nd

Street subway station during rush hour, I and hundreds of other miserable souls waited forty-five minutes for the F train. During the muffled and inaudible public announcement, I witnessed a man beside me shape-shift into a demon. His eyes turned black as onyx and a pair of horns sprouted out of his forehead. By the time the train arrived, his hoofed feet had burned grooves into the platform.

When transplants complain about our extreme climate, I shrug my shoulders and remind them New York was never known for its weather. Rich people flee to their summer homes in fancy named towns like Amagansett or Salisbury. For the rest of us, too poor to afford such luxuries, we highjack fire hydrants or consult the classifieds for vacation rentals.

Between the scorching humidity and the torturous guilt of Chad's busted knee, I needed to go to a place where there was no need for A/C or things like personal injuries. I found a cabin rental a town away from my old college stomping grounds of Amherst, Massachusetts, which sounded perfect. Cool New England nights, fireflies, and a lake were just the things to soothe my psyche. I knew I'd have more fun with company than alone. Ana was dealing with a reptilian mating emergency. Bea was busy trying to salvage her relationship with Alex. Pippa and I were college roommates; it was only natural that I enlisted her to be my Guest Number Two.

Convincing Pippa to ditch her new fiancé (a spur-of-the-moment engagement from her love-struck lover) and the real-estate game was no easy task. As long as I had known Pippa, she'd been an incessant worker and a chronic worrier—two traits that did their best to dismiss the idea.

"What if I come back and Felipe doesn't love me anymore? What if I leave and my boss finds someone else to replace me? Is it me? Am I crazy?"

For her to jump ship, she needed a good reason to leave. Fresh air and a girls' vacation didn't make the cut these days. While I was still single, fumbling through life as a wannabe writer, scratching out a living doing odd jobs and babysitting celebrities' kids, Pippa was getting her shit together. She was already halfway through her masters in Real Estate Management and tending to love's responsibilities. The only way I'd burn off her worry warts was by tickling her Achilles heel with tempting eats. I offered to make my famed mac and cheese for dinner, promised we'd eat waffles and farmer's market fresh strawberries for breakfast, and to sweeten the pot I granted her exclusive rights to the brownie bits in a pint of Ben & Jerry's. I knew if I left a trail of tasty treats, like Gretel, she would go into the woods with me. The lure worked and by the weeks end we were puttering up I-95 in my old Subaru station wagon, affectionately named the Millennium Falcon.

Two-and-a-half hours of interstate driving and we arrived at the Pioneer Valley. It was weird, being back as adults who could legally buy alcohol with valid IDs. The road led us past our old apartment complex, Alpine Commons, a haven of Nordic-looking two-story buildings.

"Still looks like the same old dump after all these years," I said.

"Remember that party where those bitches downstairs called the cops on us? It's so weird we're now grown-ups."

We followed the two-lane road of Route 9 east to Belchertown—a sleepy hamlet on the fringes of collegiate society. A right past the light at Main Street and we dipped into the mountains and cruised on a little road sipping the sandy shores of Arcadian Lake. Along the water's edge, quaint Victorian houses sat hushed with their paint-chipped shutters and screened-in porches. The blood-orange sky slowly dimmed through a thicket of maple trees.

The lakeside cabin was just as promised—an A-frame house made of timber and old lace curtains. The bathrooms were spotless. The sheets smelled like clean laundry. The only sign of life came from the occasional cricket settling in for the evening.

In the kitchen, on top of a worn farm table, was a handwritten note from the owner:

Welcome Ms. Brixi, I hope you find everything you need. The grocery store is a minute down the road. Enjoy the serenity.

Next to a vase of wildflowers was a complimentary bottle of wine, which we were more than happy to uncork.

After unpacking we headed out to the dock. On matching Adirondack chairs, we sipped our vino and smoked a celebratory joint. Every once and a while Pippa would laugh and squeeze out a monstrous fart.

"You are a beast!" I hollered.

"Ooh, it's really smelly. Hehehe."

"Does Felipe know about this farting obsession of yours?"

"Of course not! I still want him to marry me!"

For dinner we filled our bellies with couscous and marinated lamb kabobs. Once we were satiated and suitably buzzed, we said goodnight to the mosquitos and headed indoors to watch a movie. Inside the wood-paneled living room, I parked my rump on the lumpy plaid couch while Pippa scanned the wall of DVDs.

"We got *Friday the 13th*, *Harry and the Hendersons*, *Some Like it Hot*...there's a ton of stuff. What do you want?"

"Nothing too scary. We just got out of New York—I need to ease into the quiet. I'm not trying to turn into Woody Allen. Without the sirens, I'm not sure I'll be able to sleep tonight. Something funny should do."

"Ok, I've got it," she said, and slipped a DVD into the player.

It was one of our favorites: *Club Paradise*—widely discussed in our tight circle, as the most underappreciated movie of the Eighties. Jimmy Cliff's soundtrack had just kicked in when a squeak of car brakes sounded outside. A pair of headlights lit up the quiet street. After a few minutes listening to the hum of the engine running, I got the feeling the car was lingering a little longer than needed.

"What's with this car?" I asked. "It's a little strange how it's hanging out there, don't you think?"

Pippa's bloodshot gaze was suction-cupped to the television screen. I've seen this settled-in look too many times to know in a few minutes she'd be fast asleep. All I had to do was count to three.

"Huh?" she mumbled. "What car?"

"There's a car that's been idling for the last couple of minutes. I wonder what that's all about."

"You're being paranoid. It's probably nothing."

"Maybe you're right." I turned my attention back to the movie.

Several minutes later, my paranoia mounted and I grew antsy. The headlights were still there. I peeked out the front window for a better look. On the opposite side of the street was a white Jeep Wrangler with one person sitting behind the wheel. I drew shut the white lace curtains before he could see me. A second later the car drove away.

"Pippa! Did you see that? As soon as I closed the curtain, he just drove away!"

No response.

Pippa was dead asleep, her eyes closed, a pool of drool seeping out the corner of her gaping mouth.

***

Every night for the next week, precisely at eleven o'clock, the brakes of our mysterious white Jeep would announce its arrival like a whining alarm. Each time it would happen the same way. I'd draw the curtains and the damn car would zoom off into the night. I was beginning to suspect we had a real-life stalker on our hands.

"I'm not going crazy, Dad. I'm telling you—every night this guy swings around and sits there, parked right across the street. I'm creeped out. I can't sleep. This thing is giving me nightmares. So much for a vacation, right?"

"You should get some binoculars. You and Pippa do a stakeout."

"And spy on him?"

"Yeah!" he laughed. "See what he's doing."

"I don't want to know what he's doing, I just want him to stop. This isn't an episode of *Cops*, Dad. Say he *is* doing something nasty, what are we going to do—make a citizen's arrest?"

"Come on Kelly, you girls can take him."

Hearing my Dad laugh at my expense was giving me a headache.

"This isn't a joke, alright? Someone out there has it in for us. I swear it's because we're from New York. I can't tell you how many times I got pulled over in college for driving with out-of-state license plates."

"Well, honey, what do you want me to say? You should call the cops, then. You don't know who this person is, or what he wants."

"Oh my God, that's exactly what I've been saying for the past twenty minutes!"

"*Kelly*...I know you're upset. Don't take it out on me. If you're that concerned, go and do something about it. Getting mad isn't going to solve anything."

I let out a frustrated sigh. "Fine. I'll call the police now. See what this thing is all about."

"And get a pair of binoculars, I'm serious. You girls need to do a stakeout."

I promised to pick up a pair, and hung up. Afterwards I dialed the number of the local precinct. On the third ring an officer named Standstead answered the phone. Pippa and I huddled next to the receiver as I stated my case.

Officer Standstead cleared his throat. "Okay, Ms. Brixi is it? That does sound awfully suspicious. I'm going to ask you a couple of questions, if that's alright?"

"Sure thing. Shoot."

"It's standard police procedure. Do you remember the first time you noticed the vehicle in question?"

"The very first night we arrived, last Thursday night." Pippa nodded, confirming my timing of things. "Yesterday would make it a week ago."

"Alright, can you confirm the make of the car? You said a white Jeep Wrangler. Is that correct?"

"Yes."

"One last question, Ms.Brixi. I'm sorry, but I gotta ask: Have you or anyone else in your party gone through a bad breakup recently?"

That one threw me for a loop. "No. Nothing like that. We're two girls from Queens. We used to go to college up here. We came up for vacation."

In the background, I could make out the sound of rustling papers. The officer cleared his throat again. "Okay, so here's what we're going to do. I'm going to put out a memo to the night shift to be on high alert. Now, if this guy shows up at exactly the same time tonight, as I expect he will since he seems to be consistent, I want you to call this number and we'll have a squad car ready. Don't worry: we'll get to the bottom of this."

Later that night, after a comforting bowl of macaroni and cheese, Pippa and I sat poised beneath the living room window, ready for our stakeout. Earlier in the day we had hit up the local tackle-and-bait shop and bought their last pair of binoculars, on sale for forty bucks.

"My Dad would be so proud," I said with a laugh, peering through the reflective lenses.

"You got the phone number, right?"

"Right here." I flashed the scrap of paper with the precinct's number on it.

"What do you think is going to happen? This is so crazy. You know, this is something that would only happen to you."

"Hey, that's not fair! There are two of us here, in case you didn't remember. You're just as much of a magnet for weirdo freaks. *Hello*—you shacked up with a guy for days who howled like a wolf and had a black tooth."

"The black tooth? I don't remember that."

"What about the howl?"

She laughed. "Yes, that part sounds familiar."

"Good. You had me scared there for a minute...So, I really want the police to catch this motherfucker, you know." My eyes were set firmly on the street. "I mean, seriously? This is supposed to be a vacation. We shouldn't be forced to live in fear. If that was the case, I would have stayed in New York."

"Time check?" she asked.

I looked at my watch. We were seconds away from eleven o'clock. "Less than a minute to go. It's almost show time."

Pippa propped up on her knees and grabbed the binoculars out of my hands. "Oh shit, look, here he comes! Oh my God. Where's the phone? Call them, Kelly! Call!"

My hands trembled like tree branches. My fingers fumbled to punch in the numbers. A half-ring later a man picked up. His voice was out of breath.

"Belchertown Police. Officer Chandra here. How may I help you?"

"This is Ms. Brixi. I spoke with one of your officers earlier about a strange Jeep parked outside my home?"

"Yes, Ms. Brixi. Officer Standstead told us all about it. We're on it. Someone will be by your house right away. Stay where you are! Help is on the way!"

As soon as I hung up the phone, the Jeep peeled off into the night. Two minutes passed and we waited. Then a police car screamed down the road, its sirens on full blast. A few lengths behind, a second patrol car cruised by the house, scoping out the premises.

Pippa and I kept track of the time by counting our pulse while our heartbeats raced. What was going to happen when the police apprehended our assailant? Oh, how I wished we could've been in the back of the patrol car, watching the scene unfold.

Twenty agonizing minutes later the phone rang.

"It's them!" Pippa screamed. "Get it, get it."

I pounced on the phone and stood by the window. Pippa pressed up next to me to hear the conversation.

"Ah, Kelly? Officer Chandra here." So much for formalities, I was now officially on a first name basis with the Belchertown police. "I just want to tell you that you were correct about the car. We stopped a white Jeep a little ways up the road."

"Oh good. I told you it was white, right?"

"Yes, your description was spot on. Now, we questioned the person driving the vehicle."

"Who was he? Some kind of creepy stalker?"

"Not exactly..."

"Well, if he wasn't a stalker, then who the hell was he? And why has he been doing drive-bys at all hours of the night?"

There was a gap of silence. Hesitation had wormed its way into our conversation.

"Now, I don't want you to get upset, okay? I want to make sure—"

"Oh my God, it's worse than I thought. He's an escaped convict? A wanted serial killer? Ew, a rapist? You can give it to me straight Officer Chandra. I can handle it."

Pippa pinched my arm and mouthed the words, *Shut up*.

Officer Chandra took a deep breath and continued, "Ok, here goes. Turns out the driver is named Cindy Sheldon. Female, Caucasian, sixty-two years of age. She's a delivery person for our local newspaper. This was confirmed when we checked the backseat and found about twenty newspapers."

My hand hit the side of my head. Pippa dropped the phone and started hysterically giggling. Across the street there were a row of ten mailboxes. I was a moron. How could I miss something so obvious?

My nerves betrayed me and I started laughing. I picked up the phone and tried my best to regain my composure.

"So, you're serious. My stalker is a sixty-year-old delivery lady? This isn't a joke?"

"I wish it was, ma'am but I'm afraid this is no joke. But don't worry, these things happen all the time. Mistaken identities and all that."

Public puking was rough, but this was taking my humiliation to a whole new level.

"I am such an idiot. Was she all right? I hope she didn't have a heart attack."

"Well, she was a little shook up, the poor thing, but she'll be fine. Look, you can never be too sure nowadays. There are a lot of crazies out there. Best to be safe than sorry. Please don't hesitate to call us again if you need anything. I mean that. If it makes you feel any better—that was the most fun this police force has had in over fifteen years!"

posted: 2008-09-26 9:34 pm EDT

LOOKING TO SELL YOUR SOUL? I'M INTERESTED

Yes, you heard that right. While I hate the name Beelzebub, I do play the Devil in real life. I'm looking for souls with fortitude, strength (must have good pain management skills) and be willing to do my bidding 24 hrs. a day, 7 days a week for eternity.

In exchange for your soul, I will give you all the riches of the world. I'm come with cash in hand, no questions asked. If you prefer jewels or a corner office on Wall Street with 360 degree views, I can procure that too. The arrangement will be simple. I will supply an unbreakable contract for you to sign in your own blood. I will not accept applicants with recent transfusions.

Once the contract is signed and notarized by one of my minions, you will be supplied with everything you need to help me rid the world of demons, evil and monstrous human beings. God knows, Hell needs them.
Serious inquiries only.

● It's NOT okay to solicit this person with services or other unrelated interests

Wanted

His name was Carlos, a friend of a friend of a friend. Our encounter was accidental and I can't say I'll ever see him again. We met on one of those nights; you know the kind—where there's something in the air that makes your skin crawl and the back of your legs itch. Bea, Ana, and I arranged to meet up for an overdue ladies night, along with Mage—the fourth wheel of our junior-high connection. Life always managed to intervene with our schedules, so it was a rare treat to have us all together in one setting. For the first time in over a year, the weather conditions were right: Ana was in town, Bea was now single, and Mage had squeezed out a night away from her husband and one-year-old twins.

Outside of Dunkin Donuts, with fresh coffees in hand, we debated how to spice things up from our usual routine of card-playing and eating copious amounts of Indian food. I suggested that a cruise along Roosevelt Avenue would certainly do the trick. We could cop cocaine from the little old lady who sold churros out of her grocery cart, and socialize with our local transvestites. But I was ruled out and in favor of a more suitable cure for our boredom and responsible constitutions: it was decided we were going to knock around some balls at our local pool hall.

We wandered around the tree-lined streets of Jackson Heights like we did in the old days. The same prewar buildings from the nineteen-twenties—originally homes to rich men's mistresses—still twinkled with lights, but now new faces sat by windows eating their family dinners. Unlike the yesteryears of our youth, when we walked the streets with our dogs and puffed on stolen cigarettes, these days we preferred to peek through the wrought-iron gates and gaze at the manicured gardens that made up our historic district. However, some things never changed. We laughed and joked all the same, although it was gossip we really pined for—these were the things that filled in the blanks during our long naps of silence.

Ana was the first to set things swinging. "So Mage, did Kelly tell you her big news?"

"Ah, no, she did not." Mage flashed a suspicious eye. "I might be married and have kids but I'm not dead yet. What's up girl? Why you holding out?"

"I'm not holding out on anyone. Ana's hyping it up. It's nothing, really."

"Give it up, Kelly," said Bea. "We all know you're the most secretive of the bunch. She's got herself a man. You're not fooling any of us."

"Oh, do tell!" cried Mage. "My life is so boring. My tits are like udders—James now calls them his teats. You cannot imagine the palate of poop I clean up day after day. Come on Kel, I'm desperate for adult conversation. Give me some excitement, please!"

"No judging okay? His name is Karol. We met on the job. He barely speaks English. He's fresh off the boat from Poland."

"You're leaving out the best part!" said Ana. "Go on, tell her."

"He's a little young," I said with a wince.

"What's young?" asked Mage.

My cheeks flushed. "Last week he turned twenty-one."

"And that's not all," Bea hollered. "He calls her Mamma!"

Like hens in a club, I let them cluck and jab me in the name of good fun. Yes, it was true—I hadn't had sex in forever. But I still didn't understand why they turned my pathetic love life into an earth-shattering event. It's not like I was trying to be a born-again virgin. So what if I was his senior, or that he called me Mamma? At least now he could legally drink, and *boy* was he hung. My celibate spell had been broken by the body of an Adonis who fucked like a jackrabbit. If there was an Olympic sport for sex, we'd dominate the podium: Gold medals for foreplay, freestyle cunnilingus, and original choreography; silver for timing and duration spent; a bronze for technical abilities—a deduction made for youthful inexperience. The best part of our arrangement: we didn't need words, and I was tickled when he left my apartment afterwards. Take that, ladies! Ha!

Over the cackles of laughter, Mage's purse jingled. She tried to ignore it, but the chime grew louder and more insistent.

"Ugh, just shut up," she huffed. "It's James, I just know it. The man doesn't get that it's my night off. He'll never admit it, but I swear he hates being left alone with the kids." She dove into her bag and answered the phone. "Hiya, babe. No, I didn't check my messages...*What?* Fever? Oh man, you got to be kidding me. Alright, alright. I'll be home in a second." She hung up and looked at us. "Sorry ladies, looks

129

like you're going to play pool without me. Hopefully next time we meet, my kids won't be so predictable."

When people talk about Queens, the most frequently used adjective to describe the borough is "boring." Brooklyn's got its fancy brownstones, Manhattan's got Times Square, the Bronx has Yankee Stadium, Staten Island's got its rolling hills of famous landfills—and poor Queens is branded as the place people travel through on their way to the airport. On a sliding scale of cool, she sits above Staten Island and below the Bronx River Parkway. It's a shame that a borough brimming with immigrants isn't ranked higher than that. There's a simple explanation which I believe boils down to this: many Queens residents have not yet mastered the English language. They open up shops with names like Broadway Deli or Corona's Best Pizzeria. Just like their surnames, stores are named after landmarks or geographic locations, in case we forget where we're travelling or what we're getting.

The owners of BQE Billiards knew what they were doing when they put up their colored billboard next to the Brooklyn-Queens Expressway. You needed to be blind to miss the flashing sign even if you weren't driving. At night the colored balls shone like a beacon, and the closer we got to the entrance, the more I wished I'd brought my sunglasses.

"*Psst.* Sexy mamacitas. I can see your sweet tetas," a man shouted from afar. His accent was thick, like he'd just crossed the border.

Bea turned around and yelled, "Go suck it, pervert."

"Slow down Bea, it's me, Chili! Damn girl, you don't need to be so stanky!"

Out of the shadows three people emerged. Their shaggy silhouettes and knuckle-grazing gaits exuded the confidence of men you did not want to mess with. "I was just playin'," he said with a laughed. "Hold up a second and we'll play a few rounds with you girls."

Chili was latest in a long list of Bea's admirers. His most notable trait was the sad clown tattoo inked on his forearm. Ana looked unhappy as they headed our way. Her face grew pale and she laced her arms over her chest.

"Bea, I know you're on the rebound since Alex. But please, let's not do this. Chili is gross and so are his friends."

Bea waved them over with a wide smile. "He's harmless. Besides, if Kelly can have a boy toy, why can't I?"

"What does this have to do with me?" I asked.

"Her situation is different," Ana insisted. "Kelly's man works. Chili is a criminal. There's nothing harmless about him. Last time you made us all hang out, he spent the night bragging about the seven years he did for armed robbery. Doesn't that scare you? We don't want to hang out with them. Isn't that right, Kelly?"

"Ana's right. Chili isn't worth messing around with. Can't we just hang out like we said, and have it be a girls' night? His crew looks pretty ghetto."

"God, you guys are such wimps! Where's the excitement? Or did you leave it with Mage in her apartment? We'll play a couple rounds of pool together, that's all. How much trouble do you think we're going to get into?"

"I really don't know what you see in him," Ana said.

"Not everyone can have the perfect relationship like you, Ana. There's something sexy about him, something I like, okay? They're almost here. Now please, can we just drop it?"

I always wondered why the prettiest girls had the most dubious taste in men. It's a question we women have been asking ourselves for eons.

Bea was Ivy League-educated, beautiful and bright. Her list of suitors was plentiful and promising—budding doctors, lawyers, architects. Yet like so many other women who could level a man with their eyes, Bea's natural inclination consistently aimed towards the bottom of the barrel. It took Alex years of devotion to prove his weight, despite the petty drug-running and penchant for cage-fighting. But since the last flower was put on the grave of their ten-year relationship, Bea's wild streak had become increasingly dangerous.

Last month, she dragged me to a Korean mafia-sponsored barbeque where everyone ate short-ribs, drank milk chasers with jugs of Blue Label Johnnie Walker, and called themselves brother. Tonight was poised to be more of the same—hanging with ex-cons like Chili and his band of thugs.

Chili planted a wet kiss on Bea's lips and made his round on our cheeks. It was hard to tell, but I swore Chili had more ink on his skin, this time in the form of two thick, dark blue eyebrows.

" 'Sup girls," he said. "These two fools are Eddie and Carlos. Eddie lives on 85th Street. Carlos is a friend of my cousin who's just rolling through for the night."

Eddie's taut face was covered in potholes. His teeth were chipped and his bony joints poked holes in his oversized clothes. Carlos's brown skin was an odd pairing to his Viking-shaped body. He wore thick, black-framed glasses and styled his hair like a fifties greaser. Together they looked like extras on an episode of *America's Most Wanted.*

"So you're from Jackson Heights?" Carlos asked as we stepped inside the pool hall.

"Yeah, and you?"

"I grew up in the Bronx, but it's not safe there. Tomorrow, I'm heading upstate."

"That sounds nice. It'll be a big change. City life is way different than in the country."

"Not where I'm going. I already know what to expect."

He bought the first round of beers while Ana and I chose our table through the sea of green felt. Chili and Bea snuck off to a nearby table decorated in melted ashtray rings and empty beer bottles. Eddie stood by Ana, lurking around, trying to get a glimpse of her chest.

Instead of splitting into girls' and boys' teams like Ana and I insisted, Eddie made the decision when he sank his claws into Ana's waist.

"Don't try wriggling away. Me and you are a team baby."

"Ugh, let's get this over with." Ana scurried away and grabbed the first stick she could find. She channeled her frustrations through a cube of blue chalk, which she rammed over her cue tip. "The sooner we do this, the sooner I can wake up from this nightmare. I'm breaking. Everybody move out of my way."

She shoved off Eddie's groping hands and fired the first shot. Balls scattered in all directions, several landing in the corner pocket.

"Nice shot," said Eddie, drawing an arm around her waist. "It's gonna be hard to concentrate with you leaning all over the table."

"Don't touch me. God only knows where those hands have been." She peeled his arm off with a pair of pinched fingers. In the crease of his elbow were several fresh track marks.

"Yo, Chili," Eddie shouted. "Ask your girl what's up with her friend."

"She doesn't like you, Eddie," Bea shouted. "If you didn't act like a horndog, maybe she'd be less repulsed."

Eddie swiped his nose with his thumb. "Nah, she's playing hard to get, is all. Once she gets a look at this baby's arm I'm packing, she'll be a cat in heat. Ain't that right, sweetheart?"

As she leaned in for another shot, he crept up behind her and threw his lips on her neck.

Ana turned around and slapped his cheek. "Do that again and I'll ram this stick down your throat."

"Honey, you don't scare me," he said, rubbing the sting from his face. "By the end of the night you'll want to fuck me. They all do. I promise."

"I can't take this." She pressed her stick into my hand and made a beeline for the bathroom. On her way, she passed by Bea and said, "You need to fix him or I'm leaving."

Eddie polished off his beer and stormed off for another drink. Meanwhile, at the other end of the pool table Carlos and I were carrying on a polite conversation about kids.

"You gotta do what Kerry's gotta do," he said in response to a comment I made about raising a child to be bilingual.

"It's Kelly," I corrected him. "Now all I need is to brush up on my French!"

"See, Kerry, it's all about teaching a kid right. You seem like a good person, someone who won't fuck up a kid's life. "

"You had it hard?" I asked. "Parents divorced?"

He knocked two balls into one pocket and took a swig from his bottle. "You could say that."

"Mine, too. But I'm glad they split. My home life would've been hell if they'd stayed together. So, how old were you when they divorced? I was ten."

He swiveled around the table and took another shot. "Look, Kerry, you're a good girl. You don't need to hear about my fucked-up life."

Before I could answer—or correct my name for the hundredth time—my attention was drawn to the bathrooms where Eddie and Ana were in the middle of a fight.

"I said don't touch me," shouted Ana. "Why are you following me?"

"Fuck you, bitch. You act like you're all high and mighty. You know you want a piece of this." Eddie cupped his balls to prove his virility.

"What part of 'don't touch' do you not understand? Somebody want to get this animal away from me?" Ana threw her arms across her chest and looked in our direction for help.

Carlos and I put down the cue sticks and walked over. Bea and Chili followed behind a minute later.

"The lady says she's wants you to leave her alone," said Carlos, towering over Eddie's skinny frame. "I think you better do what she says."

Ana ran to my side and we hid like kids behind Carlos's tree-trunk leg.

"Fuck her," Eddie snapped. "Bitch is causing a scene for no reason. All I did was try to get a kiss out of her. This ain't your problem."

"You're makin' it my problem. Why don't you go and take a walk? Cool down a bit."

"I ain't going nowhere, Carlos. Fuck you and fuck those bitches," Eddie said, edging his chin on our direction. "I'll do whoever and whatever I like."

"Don't be like that, man," said Chili, stepping into the mix. "Not every girl is gonna want your wonder dick. Get over it and let's play some pool. Enough of this shit."

"Alright, Chili, just for you—but not for this lumberjack freak. Let's hit some balls." He winked at Ana. "It ain't over between me and you honey, you'll see."

He walked back to the table with the pool stick glued to his hand. We kept a cool distance and followed his lead. Carlos hung in the back of the pack, watching over us like an overprotective dad. None of us could see the rabid look in Eddie's eyes, or the white knuckles wound tight around his pool stick. We were too busy lowering the adrenaline in our veins to notice the butt of his pool stick aimed in our direction.

A quick twist of the wrist and BANG! Eddie bashed the stick into the wall and wailed out laughing. A millimeter above Ana's head was a hole in the drywall the size of a golf ball. We were so stunned, we froze in place, terrified to think what might happen next.

Carlos brushed us aside and swooped down on Eddie. He raised his thick fist and slammed the back of Eddie's head with it. His bony body stumbled forward two steps, then crumpled to the floor.

"Apologize, Eddie." Carlos had him pinned down, his hands wrapped around Eddie's neck.

"Fuck you," Eddie spat back.

"You asked for it."

Carlos sent his fist flying. Then another, and another.

We screamed for it to stop, to break up the situation, but our words were drowned out by the violence. Chili tried stepping in, but the two only twisted tighter into a knot and fought harder. Eddie's lip popped open and a squirt of blood slashed across Carlos's face. Carlos licked a speck that landed on his lip.

"Carlos, don't do that! He's got HIV! " Chili screamed.

"I don't care what this shit has got. I'm not afraid of dying. Some people need to be taught a lesson."

Chili dove down and heaved Carlos's heavy frame off Eddie with all his might.

"You really are a dumb motherfucker," Chili said in between breaths. "You gotta get out of here. They've already called the cops."

"Shhh, do you hear that?" said Carlos, ignoring the warning. Up from the floor came a groan of pain, then a mumble that sounded like an apology. He bent down and met Eddie at eye level. "Speak up. What was that?"

Outside red and white lights blared through the windows. Two cops stepped into the place. The manager pointed his quivering arm in our direction.

Chili was frantic and grabbed hold of Carlos. "Come on! I'll distract them and you can run before—"

"It's all good, Chili. It's supposed to happen this way."

"You're wrong. It doesn't have to go down like this. I'll say I was the one fighting."

"Enough Chili." He threw his hand in the air. "I said stop it."

Carlos hoisted Eddie to his feet and made him repeat what he was struggling to say.

Instead of an apology, Eddie heaved up and down, hysterically laughing. "Looks like we'll both be spending some time in the pen!"

The officers wasted no time in kicking both men to the floor. They slapped on the cuffs and then walked them towards the front door. We tried persuading them to let Carlos free, but they wouldn't listen. The cops said it was out of their hands; Carlos had made his decision.

On the way home, we made Chili tell us what Carlos's deal was; no man in his right mind would volunteer for prison.

Chili shook his head. "You won't believe me even if I tell you."

"Try us," said Ana.

He took a deep breath and out came a hard sigh. "Tonight was his last night as a free man. For the next seventeen years he'll be doing time for murder."

I stumbled backward. "Carlos? A murderer? No, that can't be."

"Oh, yeah it can." Out came another sigh and Chili elaborated further. "Carlos had it rough growing up: mom a heroin junkie, dad took off before he was born. His mom remarried a bunch of times. This last one—her fourth—was the worst of the bunch. Before Carlos was convicted, he worked as a bouncer for some strip clubs by the 59th Street

Bridge. Every Sunday morning on his way back home from work, he'd stop off at his mom's to make sure she wasn't still using. One of these Sundays, he let himself in and found his stepdad asleep on his recliner and his mom passed out cold on the floor of the kitchen. This wasn't the first time Carlos had seen this shit go down, but that day was different. The motherfucker got Carlos's mom good—her nose was broken and her eyes were all black and bruised..." Chili stopped to light a cigarette. "Shit...I don't like telling you girls all this."

"Go on," Bea said. "You started it, now you have to finish it."

"Alright, alright. But I'm warning you: it ain't pretty." He blew out a smoke ring and continued. "Her clothes were all ripped. Carlos flipped when he saw his mom like that and grabbed a meat cleaver, walked straight up to his stepdad who was snoring away on his recliner—one hand cupping his balls, the other still holding on to a can of beer. Without thinking, my man ran that butcher knife across his step-dad's neck and cut off the motherfucker's head. When his mom woke up a day later and found her man dead and her son covered in blood, she called the police and had Carlos arrested. Because of the fucked-up circumstances, the judge sentenced him seventeen to life. Maybe with some good behavior, my boy might actually see some sunlight."

We walked the rest of the way home in silence. No one dared say a word. I didn't sleep a wink that night, nor the few days afterwards. Sometimes Carlos's haunted memory creeps into my thoughts and rattles my dreams. When that happens, I like to pretend that night wasn't real.

posted: 2009-5-15 1:21 am EDT

Hunk on F Train with Zebra Mesh Tank Top

We were both on the F train heading towards Brooklyn last Thursday night around 7:30 pm.

You: Zebra mesh tank top, thick brown wavy mullet, cut-off jean shorts and converse high tops.
Me: Long blonde hair, red Sally Jesse Raphael glasses, golden ballet slippers, wheelchair.

We were both reading books. Mine was *Love in the Time of Cholera*, yours looked like *Harry Potter and the Sorcerer's Stone*. Our eyes met, you smiled, my cheeks blushed, then your foot accidently tripped over my wheel as you got off at the Bergen stop.

If you are reading this, I'd love to get to know you more and maybe borrow a tank top or two. Maybe we can go for coffee and read our books together. Look out for me on the F train. I'll be waiting for you.

- Location: Bergen Street
- It's NOT okay to solicit this person with services or other unrelated interests

T here are certain things you should never do when you're bored, home alone, stoned off your ass and up way past your bedtime—crank-calling the cops might be one, posting a fake personal ad online would definitely be another. You would think I'd learn my lesson and pay more attention to Craig's user agreements. It's just that when I learned Noah Enterprises had dropped their suit against me, the floodgates were opened and I felt the need to celebrate.

Honestly, I never expected for anyone to respond to my ad. Who would believe such a ship-crossing story? But to discount a whole world of weirdos would be unfair. Many of them, I was quick to find out, had crept out of their troll holes and planted letters in my email. Out of the scores of love notes that flooded my inbox in the days following my post, here are a few gems I'd like to share.

From: TonyB <Tonyb@hotmail.com>
To: cpsnp-1085453201@pers.cl.org
Date: May 15, 2009 3:11 a.m.

Subject: Hunk on F Train with Zebra Mesh Tanktop

I think I saw you on the F train. You were the girl in the wheelchair right? Did you have big tits or am I thinking of someone else? Either way, I thought you were hot.

-Tony

From: Mr Mister <mrmister@gmail.com>
To: cpsnp-1085453201@pers.cl.org
Date: May 15, 2009 8:57 a.m.

Subject: Hunk on F Train with Zebra Mesh Tanktop

Hey there hot stuff,

I don't own any mesh tank tops but I'll buy some if you want me to. I ride the F train and I think have seen you before. You live close to Smith St. stop right? Every day on your way to work you order an egg and cheese sandwich. I live across from the bodega and I watch you from my living room window. I have always wondered if those sandwiches are any good. Ronaldo behind the counter told me you like yours with extra cheese. That sounds pretty delicious if you ask me.

So are you a quad or paraplegic? Not that I have a problem with either, in fact if we get together you'll learn I have a disability too. A month ago I was diagnosed with E.D. I am thinking you might be the perfect person to help me through this. So what do you say, you think one of these days you can pick us up a couple of egg and cheese sammies (extra bacon for me please) and you can roll on through to my place and see what things we can do?

I've got an elevator, if that helps.

Looking forward to hearing from you soon.
Your bodega buddy,
Johnnie

From: Howie21 <howie21@gmail.com>
To: cpsnp-1085453201@pers.cl.org
Date: May 16, 2009 12:41 a.m.

Subject: Hunk on F Train with Zebra Mesh Tanktop

I found your ad and I think you sound like a goddess. Ever since I could walk I've had a thing for girls in wheelchairs. Maybe that's because my mom is in one. Sure you can't run, but you've got wheels so who cares right? You probably have gorgeous forearms and can do some really funky things with your legs.

While I would certainly remember if I tripped over your wheel, or those big red glasses of yours, I'm afraid I'm not your Harry Potter. But if you give me a shot, I know I can show what a great guy I am. I even have a couple of mesh tank tops I can lend you.

Would you like to go out on a date with me?

Forever yours,
Howie

From: **Shamalama** <Shamalama@yahoo.com>
To: cpsnp-1085453201@pers.cl.org
Date: May 16, 2009 2:32 a.m.

Subject: Hunk on F Train with Zebra Mesh Tanktop

Yo hizzo,
Whats the dealio? You into black guys with big dicks? Boy, do I love me some handicapped girls. They know how do the freaky deaky like nobodys business.

So whats up? You wana do dis?

From: **FrankieG** <FrankieG@gmail.com>
To: cpsnp-1085453201@pers.cl.org
Date: May 17, 2009 10:45 a.m.

Subject: Hunk on F Train with Zebra Mesh Tanktop

I can't believe it's really you. That damn wheel of yours really tripped me up. My toe is all black and blue because of you. No matter, I was distracted by your golden slippers and pretty smile. Glad you liked my tank top. I inherited it from my dad. My girlfriend loves it. She says the zebra stripes turn her into a wild beast. Any interest in a threesome?

Frankie G

And last but not least...

From: Armyguy82 <armyguy82@msn.com>
To: cpsnp-1085453201@pers.cl.org
Date: May 17, 2009 4:20 p.m.

Subject: Hunk on F Train with Zebra Mesh Tanktop

Hi,

I saw your ad posted and I noticed you are disabled. I recently lost both legs in Iraq and was recently deployed back home. It's been hard to get around, never mind dealing with the fact that I'll never walk again. Every day is a new adventure now that I am disabled. I never imagined how hard this would be. I'm sure you know it all too well. I barely go out these days. My shrink tells me I need to work on this. As you can probably guess by now, I'm not handling my life too well.

As someone who also gets around in a wheelchair, can you tell me which train stations are disabled friendly? Navigating the nyc subway system is hellish and dangerous! It is unbelievable how many stops don't have elevators or ramps. I am thinking about buying a car but they are so expensive on a decommissioned vet's salary.

Reading your ad gave me some hope. If you know of any tips on getting around, I would greatly appreciate it.

Matt

Ok, so after reading Matt's note, I was convinced I was going to go to hell. My bored exploration into the world of personal ads had brought me from men with freakish handicap fetishes to someone who really needed my help. I knew if I was going to redeem myself from such moral decrepitude, I'd best find some answers to his question. After a few hours digging online and a couple of calls to the MTA I wrote Matt back. I offer this as my penance.

From: Kelly B <kellyb@hotmail.com>
To: Armyguy82 <armyguy82@msn.com>
Date: May 17, 2009 6:11 p.m.

Subject: Hunk on F Train with Zebra Mesh Tanktop

Hi Matt,

I'm sorry to hear about your loss. I know it's hard right now, but trust me it does get easier. A good support system from your family and loved ones will help you pull through the transition of things. Believe it or not, sometimes being disabled has its perks. Think of it this way—you always get to ride in the front of the bus and get priority seating at restaurants;)

When it comes to travelling via the subway, I have found a few spots that are the easiest to get around. As you have already experienced, the nyc subway system isn't disabled-friendly. So please bear in mind that this is not a very comprehensive list. Nevertheless, there are a few stations in

Manhattan that will get you relatively close to things. Also before you head out make sure you've got a reduced fare auto-gate card to go in and out of the automatic doors, usually located next to the turnstiles. A regular metrocard won't do the trick.

In Manhattan

42nd St. Times Square: A,E,C Elevator is inside the airport bus terminal. For the N,Q,R,& 7 trains, do not even attempt using the 42nd St tunnel that connects the bus terminal to the other lines—seriously, you'll break your neck.

59th St Columbus Circle: A,B,C,D #1 trains. There are a bunch of elevators at this stop, so there are plenty of ways to connect.

Brooklyn Bridge City Hall: 4,5,6 trains have elevator access. Beware: the elevators *really* stink like piss. In fact, you probably experienced some foul odors in these metal petri dishes. Clearly, the MTA doesn't care about people with mobility challenges or mothers with strollers!

42nd St. Grand Central: 4,5,6,7 trains: Has elevators and ramps all over the place. Added bonus—unlike City Hall, this crown jewel of subway stations is guaranteed to be moderately clean. You can chalk this up to all the tourists and their incessant camera flashes. No mayor wants visitors going home with snapshots of a homeless dude taking a whiz in the background. That's just plain bad for business.

34th St. Penn Station: A,C,E and Amtrak and LIRR. There are a couple of elevators but I would try to avoid this station if you can. The place is more confusing than a Zen poem.

West 4th St: A,B,C,D,E,F,M: There is an elevator on the corner of West 3rd and 6th Ave. It's a good place for heading downtown and into Brooklyn. Watch out for the platform performers. I once got my face slapped by the leg of a salsa dancing puppet.

Good luck navigating the subways and be safe! Hope this helps!
Kelly

From: Armyguy82
To: Kelly B <kellyb@hotmail.com>
Date: May 18, 2009 11:31 a.m.

Subject: Hunk on F Train with Zebra Mesh Tanktop

Wow! Thanks Kelly! What a tremendous help you have been. Because of your list, I am actually going to get out of the house today and meet up with some old friends. You gave me the confidence I desperately needed. Maybe now I'll be able to run into you on the F train after all. I'll make sure to look for your golden ballet slippers. I have a feeling you won't be hard to miss...

Warmest regards,
Matt

posted: 2009-11-15 4:20 pm EDT

$1300/1Bdrm—Your perfect apartment is now available! (Sunnyside)

One HUGE bedroom apartment could be yours in a matter of days. The apt features hardwood floors, green courtyard views, recently upgraded kitchen and bathroom, #7 train and supermarket only two blocks away. Pets OK. What more do you need?

Text or Call Shannon to set up an appointment
(347) 806-9455

- Cats are OK – purr
- Dogs are OK - woof
- Location: Sunnyside Gardens @ 7 train
- It's NOT ok to solicit this person with services or other unrelated interests
- Fee Disclosure: no fee
- Listed By: please read above

Apartments by Owner

A few blocks south of the 36th train station in Sunnyside Queens, I stood outside a low-rise Art Deco building waiting for my real estate agent, Shannon White, to show me a prospective apartment. It was ten minutes past our appointed time and I was already thinking she had pulled a no-show. I was about to leave when I recognized her from her online profile, a head of flaming red hair barreling down the small working-class street, juggling an oversized Louis Vuitton purse and a flyaway pashmina.

"I am so, so, sorry," she shouted over the rumbling of the elevated Number 7 train. "I was closing on a deal and the paperwork sucked up too much time." Her voice had a trace of Southern belle. "You must be Kelly."

"I was about to leave," I said unamused. "I was beginning to think you weren't coming. You are ten minutes late."

She placed both palms in front of her. "I *never* stand up my clients. This was an extenuating circumstance, I swear. I get it if you want to leave, but I really want you to see this place. Still time to take a quick peek? I promise it'll be worth the wait."

My next appointment was a date with my couch and the remote control, but she didn't to know that. I checked the time on my watch. "Sure, I've got a little bit of time left, I guess."

"Great," she said and passed me a couple business cards from her purse. At the glass door of the building she abruptly stopped and tossed a manicured nail at a row of two-family homes that took up the other half of the block.

"Recognize that cute little blue house over there?"

I shook my head no.

"That's the house where they film all the Spider-Man movies. Talk about location!"

In the elevator on our way up to the top floor, Shannon gave her spiel on the apartment's dazzling amenities: spectacular light, a kitchen to die for, and a walk-in closet so big you could fit a full-size luggage set and a couple of dead bodies.

"I could go on and on about the hardwood floors and the original crown moldings, but I want to let you in on a little secret," she said as we stepped out of the elevator and onto the seventh floor. "You've got a bona fide celebrity living across the hall."

"Really? Who?" I asked, sounding skeptical.

We stopped in front of an apartment door. She put a finger to her lips then whispered, "James Franco rents the apartment across the hall because of all the late-night shooting. But no one is supposed to know he's here—so mum's the word. As you can imagine, he is *extremely* private and keeps very odd hours. Very few people in the building know about it. If they did, God only knows how many people would be knocking on his door for an autograph."

I glanced across the hall at the beige painted door while Shannon fished out the keys. The gold stickered apartment numbers were peeling around the edges. The building was clean and nondescript enough, any Joe Schmo could have lived there—shit, even James Franco. Stranger things have happened in a city of eight million. If I was some out-of-state bumpkin who had never used this celebrity tactic from my real estate days, I might have bought it. But Shannon was talking to a native New Yorker here; we don't get duped often.

"This apartment is a carbon copy of his." Shannon winked and opened the door.

The first thing that hit me was the smell of fresh paint and the bright sunlight. I had been searching for the perfect place for nearly a month and this was the first apartment that actually looked like the pictures—no wide-angle lenses were used to distort room sizes, or Photoshopped frames. For once, an apartment listing that actually delivered!

Without giving a clue to what joys rattled inside my head, I strolled across the wide, open living room to a corner window. The view was of a canopy of treetops and glimpses of a grass-covered courtyard. The corner apartment was set back, which allowed for a nice western light and envious garden views. I sat down in the seating nook, where I envisioned myself reading a cozy book. This place was exactly what I had been searching for, but I refused show it—not just yet. I wanted to milk it a little longer. She'd made me wait ten minutes in the November cold. The least I could do was make her work for her commission.

"So what do you think? Nice right?" Shannon's eager eyes searched mine for some hints. I played it cool.

"Not bad," I shrugged. "The living room could be a bit bigger. What's going on in the other rooms?"

"Come, let's take a look."

She led me into the bedroom. It had a double-sized courtyard window on one side and a walk-in closet in the other. I opened the closet and ran a finger across a shelf. I made sure Shannon saw my dissatisfaction when I flicked away an imaginary bit of dust. Two could play this cat-and-mouse game.

"I heard there was a recent crime wave in this neighborhood. Is that true?" I asked.

Shannon crinkled her nose. "I haven't heard anything like that. I think you'll find the neighborhood a very safe place. Kids still play hopscotch in the streets."

"Oh, you hear so many scary stories these days. You never know what to believe."

"Trust me—crime is nonexistent in this building. The lobby is monitored by a part-time doorman. No robber is going to get in here without someone noticing. You'll find a very tight-knit community lives here. Come, let me show you the kitchen."

We ended the tour in a narrow yet well-appointed galley kitchen. Brand new cabinets kissed the ten-foot ceiling. All the appliances were stainless steel and proudly displayed with their energy-efficient seals.

"Once the refrigerator died, I decided to redo the whole room," said Shannon. "I spent a fortune getting everything new, but look at this place. It was worth every penny."

"I didn't realize you owned the apartment. I thought you were only an agent."

"I'm both. Isn't that great?" Her freckled face beamed with pride. "This little place has done me well over these last years. I got it for a steal. Before you move in—that is if you want it, of course—I plan on putting in a dishwasher. Don't worry, I promise it'll match everything else."

I'd seen what I needed to see. It was time to drop the act and get down to brass tacks. "I must say, Shannon—as a renter who's seen her fair share of dumps, it's really quite refreshing to see an owner take such good care of things. How much are you asking again?"

"Fifteen hundred a month. That's a bargain for a place in this location. Places smaller than this are going for five hundred more, easy. And they are in *waaay* worse condition. And hey, no one else around here can say they've got a celebrity for a neighbor. You never know—maybe James Franco will have you over for coffee one day."

"Ha! I won't count on it anytime soon. So when do you need an answer? Is it alright if I take the night to sleep on it?"

She bit her lip. "Problem is—I don't want to rush you or anything—it's just I've got two other people coming over here later on this evening. So if you want it, I'd make up my mind sooner than later. Guaranteed, I'll be able to rent out the space within the next couple of days. If I were you I wouldn't hesitate."

"Hmmm...this is a big decision. Let me think, let me think..." I tried keeping my poker face while I deliberated. Up until now, my hunt had proved fruitless. It was time to bite the bullet. "You know what? Fine, I'm going to take it!"

"Fabulous! You will be happy here, I promise. Once I get the deposit and paperwork sorted out, I'll have things ready for you by the end of next week.

***

The day before Thanksgiving, Shannon and I met at the apartment and exchanged the necessary things: I gave her a cashier's check with four months' rent and she handed over the keys. We did a final tour where she showed me how to operate everything.

Over the holiday weekend, I hired movers and together we hauled boxes of books and furniture out of the U-Haul. With a few extra hands, it didn't take long for everything to fall into the place. Once the unpacking was done, some art hung on the walls, and a few plants added to the window sills, it felt like home. I christened this next chapter of my life with a bottle of bubbly and a nice long soak in some Epsom salts.

For several weeks everything seemed to be following a divine plan; life was good, the apartment was great, even work didn't seem like such a hassle. But luck has a way of falling out of favor. God had a little curveball for me and he swung it during my lunch hour. I didn't discover the damage until hours later, when my downstairs neighbor, whom I had never met, tackled me at my front door.

"Everything is ruined," cried the pint-sized Pakistani. "My wife, she is going to kill me when she gets home. I called the super but he wasn't home. I hope you plan on paying for this!"

"Whoa, whoa, slow down. What's ruined? I don't have a clue of what you are talking about, sir."

"There is water everywhere! Oh, she's going to kill me." He paced back and forth slapping his forehead like a lunatic.

"Calm down, it can't be that bad."

"Oh, it is bad. Very bad. Go, you see for yourself, lady."

I opened the door and my eyes landed on the pool of water in the middle of the living room. A stack of waterlogged paperback books bounced around my coffee table like buoys. I could hear splashing water coming from the kitchen. I ran inside, and to my horror, found myself standing in a three-inch deep tidal pool of water. I dove under the sink to shut the off the water supply. *What the hell?! No shut-off valves? Shit, shit, shit!*

With my neighbor in tow, I raced downstairs to the basement. Thankfully, Raul—the building's super, had just gotten home and taken hold of the situation. He shut off the water and went off in search of a water pump.

Meanwhile, I called Shannon to warn her of what happened. No answer. I left a message and called back later, several times. Still nothing. By the fifth call, I was pissed.

"Uh, Shannon, it's Kelly again. Look I don't want to bother you, but I've called you four times already. You need to call me back. There is a real emergency in the apartment. There are several inches of water on the floor, pooling all over the apartment. My books, the floors, the walls, my furniture...it all looks like it's going to be ruined. As I speak, the water is leaking into the neighbors' below, through their ceiling. The super said your plumber plastered over the shut-off valve under the sink? He said the plumber also welded one too many pipes, and that's why the whole thing burst. He had to tear a huge hole in the kitchen wall and wanted to know who was your plumber and if he was licensed. He's in the process of pumping the water out, but I really don't know what to do. Can you call me back and tell me how to proceed from here?"

Shannon got back to me a month later. She didn't bother to call, she did it through email.

From: Gaelicgirl77 <gaelicgirl77@gmail.com>
To: Kelly B <kellyb@hotmail.com>
Date: December 29, 2009 10:09 p.m.

Subject: Leak

Kelly,
I'm really floored at the amount of times you've called me about this leak. Have you turned into a stalker since I gave you the keys?! If I didn't call you back it's because I had more pressing matters I was dealing with. An inch or two of water on the floor is nothing. Please don't bother me with such things as they are your RESPONSIBILITY!!! I am not your goddamn maid, and I don't clean up your messes.

Shannon

From: Kelly B
To: Gaelicgirl77 <gaelicgirl77@gmail.com>
Date: December 29, 2009 11:15 p.m.

Re: Leak

Whoa, Shannon you can't really be serious? You had more *pressing issues* than a waterfall in an apartment you are renting? If I remember correctly: YOU are the LANDLORD and I am the TENANT. Leaks of any kind that are a result of shoddy plumbing are your responsibility. I have laid out $1,200 just to get the walls and leak fixed. I used the plumber and paint skimmer Raul hires for the people in the building. I will be deducting this money from next month's rent check.

As for my stuff and the neighbor's apartment below, I think you should pay for these damages. After all, it was your plumber who caused the leak in the first place. The floors still need to be redone as they are beginning to grow mildew in some spots that still haven't dried up yet. You need to get someone in here to fix this. The apartment is barely livable at this point. I don't see how you'd want the damage to linger much longer than this.

Kelly

From: Gaelicgirl77
To: Kelly B <kellyb@hotmail.com>
Date: December 30, 2009 1:58 p.m.

Re: Leak

It would be wise of you not to threaten me. I want to see January's rent check paid in full by the 1st of the month or else I will be forced to call the authorities. Neither myself, nor my plumber, had anything to do with the damage in the apartment, stop saying we did. If you wish to seek a bailout from anyone for the leak, the walls, or the goddamn floors, bring it up with the co-op board of the apartment building. Like I told you before—YOUR MESS IS NOT MY FUCKING PROBLEM!!!!

From: Kelly B
To: Gaelicgirl77 <gaelicgirl77@gmail.com>
Date: January 1, 2010 7:23 p.m.

Re: Leak

Shannon,

I sent out January's rent check minus the $1200 for water damages to your P.O. Box address. Due to the rotting wood, I was forced to hire someone to fix the floors. He told me if the mold was to go on any longer it would be a major health code violation. His estimate is $3,100 because he needs to rip the whole floor up in the kitchen and living room. He will begin work next week. As a result of laying out the funds for these repairs, I won't be sending you another check until the 1st of April. That should even us up.
Happy fucking New Year.

From: Gaelicgirl77
To: Kelly B <Kelly B@hotmail.com>
Date: January 1, 2010 11:58 p.m.

Re: Leak

I knew you were going to turn out to be a little bitch. You owe me the remaining rent in FULL!!! If you refuse to pay, I will go in there and throw your ass out. I am not joking. You would not be the first one I've had to kick out of the apartment. So let me be perfectly clear--I want to see a $1,500 dollar cashier's check in my P.O. box by the end of the week, or I will call the police on the grounds of trespassing. Oh yeah, I'll be suing your ass for every goddamn penny.

***

I was shocked at how a seemingly well-adjusted person like Shannon could turn into a raving lunatic bitch over a stupid leak? Stuff like this happens all the time to landlords, that's why they have insurance. Her odd behavior had me questioning everything. All I knew was if I had to lay out any more cash on this money pit apartment, I'd be broke by the end of the week.

My mother, who was so concerned with my frantic state, put me in contact with an old family friend and lawyer, Sean Kearny, to help me sort through things. I almost cried when he offered his legal guidance for free. Over a cup of coffee in the comfort of his glass office, Sean doled out his professional opinion.

"Your landlord has no legal grounds to throw you out or take you to court. Anything having to do with faulty construction in a rental unit lies squarely with the owner of the apartment, not the renter. A judge would immediately look at this case and throw it out of court."

"You don't know how relieved I am to hear you say this. I've been so stressed out, I've been losing so much sleep."

"This landlord of yours is blowing a bunch of hot air in the hopes you will get scared and drop the whole thing. But as your lawyer, I urge against this. We need you to recoup those damages," he said adjusting his onyx cufflinks. "Here's how we should proceed: send me over a copy of all the construction invoices. Do not give her any rent until April and make sure to pay by check. You need to keep a paper trail of all your financial transactions with her. If she sends you another threatening message, forward me the email and I will contact her on your behalf. Meanwhile, I'll draw up something and get the ball rolling on a countersuit. At the very least we need to get your money back."

This was the best news I had heard all month. Sure, my floors were blackened with mold and half of my stuff was in the garbage, but it looked like the tide had finally turned in my favor. Legally speaking I was in good shape. On the way home, I made the executive decision and picked up a nice porterhouse steak for dinner. It was time for a little celebration.

Loaded up with groceries and a fine bottle of red wine, I dumped my shopping bags on the floor in front of my apartment. I slipped my key into the lock. Something was off;

it refused to budge. *What the fuck?* There were fresh scratch marks on the lock.

"Oh come on, you've got to be kidding me. Seriously?!"

I popped the key back in, hoping some magical lock fairy had come and fixed everything. I tried twisting it again, nothing. *That bitch! She must've changed the locks while I was at work. How dare she!*

The blood rushed to my head. I cupped an ear to the door. There were people in there, rifling through my stuff!

I banged on the door so hard the bones in my hand hurt. "Shannon, you have no right to do this. Open up. Let me in, goddamnit."

The voices stopped and paused in silence. I pressed the buzzer hard with my thumb and banged even louder.

"Whoever you are, you have no right to be in there without my permission. I'm giving you a minute before I call the police and my lawyer!"

Behind me, a door creaked open. My fiery eyes were ready to fry somebody's face off. I spun around and shouted, "Just stay out of this and mind your own business." Then I registered who was standing a few feet away from me. I blinked a couple of times as if I was seeing a hologram of a famous person. "James Franco?"

The actor stepped into the hallway. He had on a bathrobe and a pair of ratty sweat pants.

"Something the matter?" he asked, casually tossing a hand through his rumpled bedhead. "I heard the banging. You woke me up."

I stuttered. "Um...yeah... sorry about that. See—the woman who rented me this apartment is a fucking psycho. She must have changed the locks on me while I was at work.

Now she's in there going through my stuff." My mind was having a hard time processing everything. "Wait a minute...you actually live here? I thought my landlord was bullshitting me."

"Yeah, I live here. It's alright," he shrugged. "So what's up—you call the police yet?"

"No," I said, which reminded me to bang on the door again. "But I *will* call the *police* if someone doesn't open the door this goddamn minute!"

A moment later, the lock clicked and the door swung open. Instead of coming face to face with Shannon as I'd hoped, a couple of suits wearing deadpan looks on their pale white faces stared at us from across the threshold. The man smelt like expensive cologne. The woman beside him had no makeup on and wore cheap-looking shoes.

James Franco smirked and scratched his head again. "Not your landlord?"

"Most certainly not," I said staring at them with curiosity.

"May we help you?" the man asked, looking confused.

"Uh, I might ask you the same question. Who the hell are you? And what are you doing in my apartment?"

I tried pushing my way in, but the man swung his arm across the entrance like a barricade.

"I'm sorry but you must be mistaken," he said. "I'm afraid you cannot come in."

"*Excuse me?*"

"This apartment is a foreclosed property of the bank."

"Shit. That sucks," said James.

I closed my eyes and shook my head in agony. I wondered who I'd crossed in a past life to be this cursed.

"What you are saying is impossible. The owner of the apartment, Ms. Shannon White, rented me the space two months ago. See, I even have a set of keys that worked, before you changed the locks." I jingled the set in front of them. "May I see some form of identity please before I go ahead and call the police?"

"Very well." The man procured a business card from his wallet. It read Phillip Houff, V.P. of mortgage lending at Americorp Bank.

"You have a driver's license to back this up? I want hers, too."

"Is this really necessary?" asked the woman. Her voice was thick with irritation. "Clearly you—"

"—Uh, clearly you don't understand I'm ready to punch in this door right now. So if you don't want any black eyes, I'd say ID's are very necessary, sweetheart. With James here as my witness, you people are in *my* apartment going through *my* things. Best fork it over, honey."

She glared at her boss with an incredulous look. He put a sympathetic hand on her shoulder. "It's alright, Hilda. Give the woman your ID and business card, please."

James made me pass their information his way once I was done with my examination. He glanced down at Hilda's driver's license and scrutinized her picture like a traffic cop.

"It says here you're thirty-one." He procured a frayed toothpick from the pocket of his threadbare terrycloth robe. "You should really think about getting a new job. 'Cause, no offense, but you could look so much younger than this." He cocked a sideward smile and handed back the driver's license.

"I'll think about it," she said. Her cheeks turned a shade of cherry-pink as James's brushed a finger against her hand.

I shot him a dirty look. "Done fraternizing with the enemy?"

Out came his famous Cheshire grin. "I guess," he said.

I turned my attention back to the banker. "Mr. Houff, or whatever your name is, I want some answers. Why am I locked out of my own apartment?"

Mr. Houff cleared his throat. "As I tried explaining before, this apartment belonged to a Mr. and Mrs. Simon Pullion. They defaulted on their mortgage seven months ago and the bank foreclosed on the property. Legally speaking, it is you who is trespassing, not us."

"So are you telling me the woman who rented me the apartment, is a crook and I got scammed?"

"Damn, you just got played, girl." James and his new female friend stifled a few laughs.

That was it. I swung around to my nosey neighbor and said, "You know what? I never thought I'd be saying this, but can you please go away? You are more celebrity than I can handle for one day."

"Well, if you're gonna be like that." He turned around, his ego visibly hurt. "I was only trying to help. I've got class in a couple of hours, I should be studying anyway. See ya around...or not." He snickered and disappeared into the dark quarters of his mystery apartment.

With James out of sight, the woman's smiling face snapped back to its original shape of a half-eaten prune.

I pressed on. "There was a leak and I want to make sure everything is okay. The least you can do is allow me to check on my things. I promise I won't do anything stupid. What do you say? Normally, I'm not such a nutcase." My eyes welled up with tears. "I can't believe this is happening to me. This might be the worst two months of my life."

The banker dropped his arm. The stern lines on his face lightened. "Come inside. I'll call the bank and do my best to sort this thing out."

I sighed in relief when I saw everything was as I left it. Then a feeling of devastation washed over me. I thought I was going to be sick. The place was an absolute wreck. Everywhere I looked something was destroyed.

Overflowing black garbage bags oozed like tar pits. I was never going to recoup the money I had spent on the place. I was a victim of an epic scam. I was a New Yorker, these things happen to other people. I never saw it coming. How could I be so naïve?

At my rotting dining room table, Phillip shared some vital information that he thought I should convey to my lawyer. Shannon had been investigated by the FBI for over a year. My place was the seventh foreclosed apartment she'd rented illegally across five states. Usually victims like myself would find out about the scam months later, when the bank finalized a sale on the apartment. The new owners would move in and the whole thing would come crashing down on the innocent renter like a hammer to the head. Shannon's belligerence over the repairs should have been my first clue. If it hadn't been for the flood, the bank wouldn't have known I was living there, and Shannon would have milked me for much more than I'd already spent on plumber bills.

In total, I lost close to $10,000. It was a costly mistake that I swore from that night on I would never fall for again. Because of the extensive expenses I shelled out for the apartment's upkeep, the bank granted me a two-week grace period to find another place. My lawyer made numerous attempts to contact Shannon, but not surprisingly, she had disappeared without leaving a forwarding address. I imagined she had already moved on to another unsuspecting victim. Word got around that the FBI's investigation had been thwarted once again.

Lucky for me, a friend living around the corner was leaving New York to pursue acting in L.A. She had a cute little place and I was able to move in right away. I never had any run-ins with James Franco again, despite keeping an eye out for his scruffy face at our local bodega. For now, I like to think even if we did across paths again, he wouldn't remember me anyway. 'Tis life in the big city—a new neighbor today, a stranger tomorrow. The concrete jungle can be cruel in so many ways.

Dear Craig

It's been so long since I've written, I thought it was time to catch up. Life here is moving at a rapid pace. You'll be happy to learn after playing the victim in a real-estate scam (you should really be more vigilant about checking those listings!) I moved into a new apartment that occasionally stinks like burnt meat. Right now I am between jobs, hoping to land something steady. To keep up the rent, my living expenses, and the thousands I lost in the scam, I've been doing a lot of handyman work: grouting showers, refinishing old furniture, repainting musty basements, those kinds of things. It's a lot of grunt work and boy, am I beat. All I want to do at the end of the day is eat a bowl of gooey mac and cheese, snuggle up with my recently rescued kitty named Mia, and conk out while reading a good book. The reality is, I'm eating ramen by the gallons and crying myself to sleep. I believe experts are calling this a quarter-century crisis.

Life was going good there for a while. I landed a couple of great jobs, some—if you can believe it—involved constructing a theater and gold leafing, of all things! Then my well of funds dried up after the Hoover fucking Dam broke in my apartment and as they say, the rest is history.

While I'm still waiting for my knight in shining armor to come rescue me, all of my friends are getting married or busting out babies. I'm getting tired! Where is this guy already? As the years go on, it gets harder to go out there and date—especially when you feel like a fat, greasy turd on a chopstick. Ugh, I'm such a lame self-defeatist, even I hate me. And no, I'm not about to get my period, if that's what you're thinking!

In my defense about the dating thing, I have my lowered standards; and still the prospect of finding a decent human being is so B-L-E-A-K. I'm noticing a disturbing pattern of guys I'm attracting these days: cab drivers who slip me their phone numbers on the back of taxi receipts, Haitian guys with the name Jean-Baptiste (I swear, I've gotten hit on by three this past month) and Wall Street types who want to date artsy girls for the novelty. I'm not sharing all this with you as an invitation for you to set me up on another blind date—that would be too much at this point. I'm only mentioning all this because I'm lonely and wondering if this is as good as it gets. Am I going to turn into one of those old ladies with a hairy chin and cankles so swollen she can barely walk, who spends her days feeding feral cat colonies? I already gained a whole seven pounds because every night I'm drowning my disappointments in tubs of ice cream. If I keep this up, I'll have legs the size of an elephant's.

So there you have it, Craig; welcome to my world of the good, the bad, and the goddamn ugly. Pass me a spoon would ya? I've got a pint of Chunky Monkey to finish up...

I hope all is well in your world. Thanks for listening.
Your old friend,

posted: 2010-03-03 3:33 pm EDT

Wanna sleep over? I've got a spare tanning bed

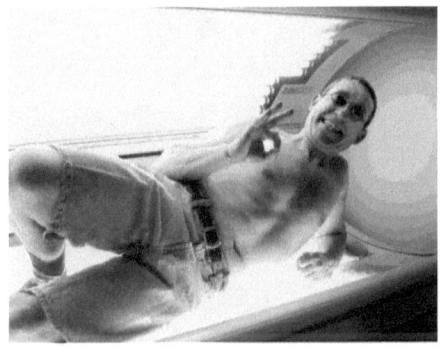

Got a cold? Need more Vitamin D? Or maybe you're just curious about what it's like to get your freak on inside a tanning bed. Hey, I'm single and willing, if you're down for that sort of thing.

Not sure? Don't worry. Schedule an appointment and check out the tanning bed for yourself before committing to anything. The tanning bed is located inside an extremely sterile environment which also doubles as my living space. So for anyone looking an interesting evening or simply a hygienic way of getting rid of that lingering cold for good, give me a ring.

My name is Adam and I can be reached at (718) 333-0055.

- Location: Forest Hills, NY
- It's NOT okay to solicit this person with services or other unrelated interests

Rants

very person at some point wishes they had a remote control to direct their life. Fast forward to the good times, pause to see that thing we missed, stop for when we've had enough, hit play for when we want to be in the thick of things. For me, I'd like the power to rewind and delete. Push the button, review a scene, and remove the file from ever seeing the light of day. In my short life on this planet I've experienced embarrassing flashes, stressful moments, elated highs and pathetic lows—each of them in its own imperfect way has made me smile, cringe, cry, seethe, or a combo of them all, depending on the specific memory. Yet for all of the tragic mistakes I've stumbled out of, I always held the belief the big cheese upstairs was trying to teach me things. As if God wanted me to know the short-sidedness he weaved into my DNA was put there for a good reason. But if he ever gave me a remote and said, "Go ahead, it's yours to use just this once", I wouldn't hesitate. I'd slam that delete button right over Adam Leiber's face.

Adam and I shared a mutual friend named Steve, an old cube mate from my days in publishing. Over endless reams of demographic statistics, Steve would tell me all about his friend and how one day I had to meet him. Adam worked on

Wall Street as a stockbroker for a Swiss investment bank. Most notably, on his first week on the job he transferred thirty million dollars into the wrong bank account. "The kid is crazy," I remember Steve saying. "The only reason Adam still has the job is because of the American Disability Act. Can you believe he lied and blamed the whole fiasco on a debilitating case of dyslexia? Who is going to challenge that?"

I had the pleasure of meeting Adam for the first time during an after-work outing with friends. Jello shots were involved, as was a whole lot of '80s karaoke—a Molotov cocktail of calamity. The night had turned ugly and by eleven o'clock I was drunk, dancing on the flashing checkered floor of the Culture Club—a denizen of bachelorette parties, recently divorced men, and a fresh out-of-college workforce sweating off their happy-hour binges by belting out songs like "Little Red Corvette."

A long time ago I read an article titled, "How to Read a Person in Thirty Seconds." A crinkle of the eye, a flared nostril, a twitchy wrist—these were all one needed to gauge a stranger's personality. Too bad the article didn't list sobriety as part of its equation. Had Adam and I met a couple of drinks earlier, I would have watched out for his beady eyes and said "No" in three different languages. Nevertheless, in my skewed state I found him short and seemingly sweet. He had dimples and a good head of hair, the kind of attributes his grandma would probably mention on line at the grocery store to any woman standing within five feet.

"He's such a nice Jewish boy," she'd lament. "I don't understand why he can't get a date. Did I mention he works in finance? Here, let me show you his picture. Look at that smile! He's a real keeper."

What she would fail to mention, through little knowledge of her own, was that when her grandson wasn't misappropriating millions of dollars, he was a weekend warrior who hit the singles scene with a vengeance.

Our first conversation began at the bar while I was navigating my mouth around the little pink umbrella in my cocktail. The Jello shots I was wrangled into consuming an hour earlier had kicked in and my motor skills had slipped significantly, like a bad transmission. As I struggled to get hold of an evasive straw without poking my eye out, Adam slid up next to me and attempted his first move.

"So, you're kinda hot. What do you say we get out of here and go back to my place?"

"Did you just say pizza?" I shook my head, misreading what he said. "I don't know of any good places around here. You?"

"I'm trying to tell you that I think you're hot," he shouted over the music. "How about I get your number and we go out on a date?"

INXS wailed in the background; the good vibes were flowing. In my inebriated state, I asked the bartender for a new straw and a napkin.

"What the hell. Give me a pen and I'll write it down..."

The next morning when I rolled into the corporate offices of the publishing giant where I worked, my brain ached as if a thousand hooves had trampled my head. Even after two jumbo cups of coffee, my bloodshot eyes looked like they'd come out of last night's blender. Everything hurt, even the overhead fluorescent lighting.

I was making the agonizing walk to my desk when my friend and fellow colleague Teresa tackled me in the hallway. "You didn't give your phone number to that guy Adam last night, did you? Cause if so, you're gonna want to hear what he said about you after you left. It wasn't pretty."

"Teresa, I feel like shit. Do I really need to hear this right now? Can't you see I'm suffering? Wait a minute...How can you be so spry when you left the club after me?"

She smiled and her cheeks shimmered with a little too much blush and foundation. "Ambien and Diet Coke. Does the trick every time. Now listen up, this is important."

She leaned over, her lips practically grazing my ear. The smell of her heady floral perfume made me slightly queasy. "I overheard Adam talking to Steve, saying something like, 'I don't care if she's nice. All I want to do is take her skinny body and bang her doggy-style on top of my desk.'"

"Ugh," I groaned. "Ok, now my hangover is fifty times worse. Thanks, T, I guess there's another fool I won't be wasting my time with."

"That's not all. When I told him he was a creep and I'd heard everything he said, he called me a *C-U-Next-Tuesday!*"

I scratched my head. "Sorry, I'm not processing."

She patted me on the shoulder. "Finish the rest of your coffee and spell it out. He's a real jerk. I'd watch out for him, if I were you."

I took Teresa's advice, and over the course of the week, Adam's fifteen phone calls went to voicemail. When I grew tired of checking my messages, I made Steve tell him I had gotten back together with an ex-boyfriend.

That was the end of our story...or so I thought.

Fast-forward ten years. Adam and I ran into each other again, this time in Englewood, New Jersey—the site of Steve's big, fat Jewish wedding. In the spell between our distant meetings, Adam and I had become silent enemies; he scorned me for refusing to date him, I grew to hate everything he represented. Just the mere mention of his name sent my eyes swirling into the back of my head.

The day of the wedding, I watched Adam be a dutiful groomsman, making speeches and smiling for the cameras when needed. I had managed to avoid him by strategic crowd placements for most of the day, but as the festivities wore on, ducking him proved more difficult. He eventually tracked me down at the cold hors d'oeuvres buffet when I was hungry and at my most vulnerable. I pretended I hadn't seen him make a beeline for me by casually grazing over a platter of raw shrimp, under the watchful eye of a large swan ice sculpture. My mind screamed, *Quick! Grab food and get the hell out of here as fast as you can!* I threw a fistful of pink crustaceans on my plate and looked for the best means of escape. I'd barely got a foot from the buffet when Adam stepped in my way.

"I see what you're doing, Kelly. You've been running away from me all day. What do you say: A truce?" He pulled a white napkin from his breast pocket and waved it. "Can we start over? Hi, my name is Adam. You must be Kelly."

He extended a hand and I ignored it. Instead, I popped a raw shrimp in my mouth and avoided eye contact while I picked over the food on my plate. "Spare me the niceties,

Adam. I know you hate me for dissing you. Steve told me everything you said."

"Hate you?" He sounded genuinely hurt. "I'm disappointed, maybe. But hate you? Never. That was such a long time ago, I don't see any reason why we can't get over it. I would have apologized if you'd just given me the chance. I know I said some disgusting, chauvinistic things back then, and for that I'm sorry. But I've changed. You'll be happy to know I'm no longer on Wall Street. That should say something."

"OK. So if not Wall Street, then what are you doing?" I asked, unenthused.

"I'm a cop now, working for the NYPD." He swung a proud hand on his hip.

I looked up at him. "You? A cop? I find that hard to believe."

"Wanna see my badge?"

"No, not really."

"Come on Kelly, why don't you let me take you out to dinner?" he pleaded. "Let me prove I'm not the sleaze bag you believe."

"I'm not sure I like the idea."

A waiter refreshed a tray of oysters and I reached over to grab some. At the nearby station I spotted an old colleague. I found my perfect excuse to hightail it out of there.

"Nice seeing you again, but I've got to go. There's someone over at hot apps that I've been meaning to catch up with. Good luck with the whole cop thing. See you in another ten years, I guess."

Adam grabbed hold of my arm. "Dinner. That's all I'm asking. If you still think I'm an asshole afterwards, I'll leave you alone and I swear you'll never hear from me again. Please, I want to make things up. Will you let me do that for you?"

"You *really* promise to leave me alone for good if I don't like you?"

He raised two fingers. "Scout's honor."

My eyes wandered over to the dance floor: Wives boogied down in sequin ball gowns; their husbands watched on, smiling, their skin as tanned as leather. Maybe it was all the love Steve and his beautiful bride were radiating, but there was something about Adam that made me want to believe him.

"Fine," I grunted. "One date, and that's it. And I'm choosing where we eat."

A few days later we met up for Indian food on the Lower East Side. I wanted to see if he could handle the curry. To my surprise, not a drop of sweat beaded on his forehead, even after I ordered the hottest items on the menu. In fact, he was such a good sport I was willing to forgive the bad first impression and give him another go at things. By the time we were planning our third date, Adam had taken to calling me several times a day.

"Hey you, how's it going? You'll never believe what I ate for lunch today."

In the background, faint sounds of police sirens wailed. Gusts of winds howled in my ear.

I yanked the phone away. "Are you on the job right now?"

"Yeah, I'm on roof at the Ravenswood Projects. Why?"

" 'Cause it sounds like gunshots are going off in the background. Are you sure talking on the phone while on-duty is such a good idea? I'd never forgive myself if you got injured."

"Kelly, stop worrying. I'm a cop. I'm trained to handle danger. Look, I need to warn you about something before our next date."

"Does it have anything to with all those bottles of Purell you're always using? When we split that cab ride the other night, you squirted your hands like, fifty times. Part of me wanted to ask if you were OCD."

He laughed. "If you could see the filthy places I work in, you'd be lathering your hands with sanitizer, too."

"But we were in a cab, after eating a fancy dinner—not some grimy hallway."

"Look, we're getting off topic." He sounded annoyed. "I'm gonna need to jet in a second. Things are getting a little hectic downstairs. I just wanted to say: Don't be surprised when you see me that I'm the color of a Milky Way."

"As in the candy bar? What do you mean? What happened? Are you alright?"

"Let's just say I was fighting off a cold and spent a little too much time in my tanning bed."

A personal tanning bed? Is that what he just said?

"I can't go into it now," he continued. "But I'll see you tonight at the theater. Eight o'clock okay?"

"Alright, I'll keep my eyes peeled for an orange freak. Don't get yourself killed down there."

***

Under the marquee lights of a local movie theater, Adam rolled up in a down parka looking like a burnt orange peel. I put my gloved hand over my mouth and tried hard not to laugh.

"Wow, you weren't kidding when you said dark! How many minutes were you in that thing?"

"I set the timer for ten minutes, but I got out after fifteen." He wandered to a nearby parked car and checked out his reflection in the windshield. "Is it really that bad? Come on, you can tell me."

"Looks like you were on vacation," I lied. "Anyway, the color will die down in a couple of days. I've never heard about killing colds with tanning beds before. You sure that's a real thing?"

"Of course it's real. It is all about the vitamin D, baby."

"But those things are cancer boxes, haven't you heard?"

"Just a myth," he said dismissively. "Hey, what do you say we ditch the movie and get something to eat? I'm starving. My place is right around the corner. We can get some pizza and watch a little TV."

"So long as you promise not to get too frisky. I know it's the third date but I'm not quite ready, if that's okay. Besides, I've got to be on the job early tomorrow, so I won't be staying too late. If you're okay with that, I'm game."

"Of course. One of these days I'm going to have to come down and see you work. I bet you look really sexy in all that construction soot."

"Covered in paint and sawdust? Construction sites are the *furthest* thing from sexy. If you don't believe me, I'll introduce you to Miguel. His farts smell like rotting enchiladas."

Adam laughed and threw an arm around my shoulder. "OK, I take that back. I still want to keep my appetite. I'm

185

excited you're coming over. I can't wait for you to check out my place."

In fact, I was very curious to inspect his apartment. In the two times we had gone out I'd become convinced Adam suffered from some form of obsessive compulsion. Even though he denied it, he was always bathing his hands in sanitizer, and he confessed to taking a shower at least three times a day. My fantasies about his apartment had it full of organized boxes, color-coded closets, and coffee-table books squared off at precise right angles. What I discovered when I stepped through the door was more casual than I expected. There were no bulk-sized bottles of Purrell laying around, only an innocent pair of pants hung over an armchair in the living room. In the kitchen there were a couple of dirty glasses in the sink and some breadcrumbs scattered on the counters. I was disarmed. The place was almost *too* messy. I wondered if he strategically strewn those crumbs on my behalf.

"You are going to love my bathroom," he said as he walked me past his bedroom.

The two of us squeezed inside and mused over his array of body lotions and white orchids. He leaned in and kissed me. A minute later, he tossed his shirt in the hamper and led me to his bedroom. The moment my foot made contact with his clam-shaped tanning bed, I should have known the night wasn't going to end well.

After some heavy petting I came up for a breather. "It's getting pretty late. I should really call a cab and go home. Better stop while we're ahead."

He propped himself against the headboard. A patch of dry skin curled up from his shaved chest. "A cab? What are you, crazy? If anything, I'll drive you. Seriously, you don't have to leave. If it's because of the sex thing, I meant what I said earlier, we don't have to do anything. I just like being around you, sharing your company."

"I don't know. I feel a little funny."

"Don't be silly. If you feel that weird, I'll sleep on the couch and you can have the bed. Unless you want to sleep in my tanning bed?"

I glanced over at the gray tin can and shook my head. "It looks mighty claustrophobic in there. I think I prefer your bed."

"Then that does it. Let me get you some pajamas to sleep in."

Together in a couple of college t-shirts, we watched a little late night television like an old married couple, and dozed off to sleep. Hours later I awoke to Adam thrashing around, kicking the sheets off the bed, and fluffing his pillow while he rubbed his neck.

"Are you up?" he whispered. "Is it hot in here? Are you up? Kelly, you awake?"

He nudged me until my eyes opened. I leaned over the bed and reached for the glass of water that I had placed on the floor earlier. Under my side of the bed was Adam's six-gauge revolver. It took me a moment to register where I was and why I was being summoned from the dead.

I took a long sip and looked at Adam, who was seated at the edge of the bed.

"You hot? I'm hot. Is it hot in here?" His questions were on a loop. "Maybe you should go home? What do you think? You want me to drive you home? I think that would be best. You're hot right?"

I made out the time on the clock. It read 4:49 a.m. "I have to be at work in three hours. You're serious—you want to kick me out? Is that what you just said?"

"What?" He paused. "No...well...maybe...yeah, maybe you should go. I'm going to jump in the shower and I'll drive you home. I'll be out in two minutes."

The bathroom door slammed and I heard the sound of water running. Furious, I leapt out of bed, threw on my clothes, and called for a cab. I wanted to be gone before he finished, but his expertise in showering had him out in less time than it took for me to get hold of a dispatcher. He stepped out of the steamy bathroom fully clothed with a set of car keys in his hand.

On the ride home Adam did all the talking. He kept going on about how sorry he was and asking if I noticed how hot his place gets.

"It's no excuse, I know," he moaned. "I hope you can forgive me tomorrow, when you see how much comfier you'll be in your own bed."

Oh, how I wished I'd had a rag doused in chloroform so I could have shoved it down his throat. "Can you stop talking? Your lame reasoning is giving me a headache. Maybe if you're quiet I can forget this night ever happened."

I had ten minutes of blissful silence; then we arrived in front of my building. Adam, the consummate gentleman, insisted on escorting me all the way up to my apartment.

I pinned myself into the furthest corner of the elevator and stared at Adam's crusted, sunburned face. I felt the loathing foam up from my feet. I couldn't contain myself anymore. I had to say something. I broke my silence by asking him a question I was burning to hear answered.

"Let me ask you this: are we here, right now in this elevator because I didn't fuck you tonight?"

Adam looked taken aback, as if my sharp tone mortally wounded his sense of dignity. "No, of course not. How can you honestly ask me that? You felt how hot it gets in my apartment—you even said so yourself, when we were in bed. I have lots of trouble sleeping. It has nothing to do with you. Please, let's not turn this into a bigger deal than it already is."

"Whatever," I hissed. "You are an asshole for convincing me to stay in the first place. This is not how you treat people."

The elevator opened and I pulled out my keys. "Don't bother coming out. I've got it from here."

He propped the door open with his hand. "I really like you a lot, Kelly. Please tell me this isn't it, we will go out again, right? I've got a lot of feelings for you. Please..."

I laughed and pulled his hand away. "Go out with you again? You've got to be kidding me. Remember your promise—don't ever contact me again. I'm serious."

Moral of the story: Some things, like first impressions, can never be undone. Now if I only knew how to figure out this remote. There's got to be a delete button somewhere.

posted: 2010-07-11 4:16 pm EDT

Found Bird (Queens)

If you lost a bird in the vicinity of Sunnyside Queens on July 5th, please contact me. It is yellow with bright orange cheek patches. I was told it is a cockatiel. I can't tell the sex, but he/she seems very friendly. I bought him a cage and he is eating well. I would love to get him/her back home asap.

If you think this is your bird, contact me at the link above. My name is Kelly.

- Location: Sunnyside, Queens
- It's NOT okay to solicit this person with services or other unrelated interests

Community

W hat makes people animal magnets? Is it the perfume? Pheromones? Something in the DNA? I don't make a habit of walking around with treats in my pockets, and yet stray animals flock to me as if I was Saint Francis. There must be an invisible sign dangling from my neck that only animals can read. It says something like this: *Come with me and I'll feed you for eternity*. I don't speak feline, but I'd bet the world's last cup of coffee my adopted cat saw my sign and thought, "*Hmmm, now she looks like a good candidate. Maybe if I look cute enough she'll take me in and feed me*."

You see, suckers aren't born; we are molded out of wet mushy clay.

All it takes is one look into a bottomless pool of sad eyes and the next thing you know you're schlepping home ten-pound bags of kitty litter. My cat understood this, and now she spends her days in a cozy home filled with unlimited treats, ounces of cosmic catnip, food on demand, and endless petting. If only humans could be so lucky.

But life for her wasn't always so rosy. Her youth was spent surviving on the cold city streets, scavenging for scraps of food and wayward rodents. It was a hard-knock life and she was determined to change her destiny. Our first encounter happened one evening as I shuffled home from work like the rest of the cattle of commuters. As we slowly dredged our way up from the subterranean tunnels of the NYC subway, this skinny little cat with lime green eyes and a dirty white coat watched us from the top of the stairs. She sat in silence, as if she was carefully selecting her perfect victim from an endless lineup of panting people. The moment my foot hit the street above, she cried out and nudged my knee. *Pretty cat*, I thought, and I scratched the top of her head. The next thing I knew, she was following me on my five-block journey home. Hopping on and off the curb, she trotted by my side, occasionally pausing to rub her purring body against my clothes to mark her territory. Every day for an entire month, this was our routine, until one day I gave up and said, "Alright cat, today's your lucky day. You're going to get what you want. Time to come home. Since you're mine now, your name should be Mia. So, let me guess: You're hungry."

When people ask how I got my cat, I say she chose me. When they ask about my bird, I tell them it arrived on my windowsill, hungry and shivering.

This little parcel flew into my life exactly one year to the day after Mia became domesticated. I was in the middle of folding laundry when I was interrupted by an incessant chirping outside my bedroom window. The noise was too foreign to be the song of a common city sparrow or a mockingbird. No, whatever was making this pitiful racket was a foreign creature begging for my help.

Saint Francis to the rescue again.

I peered through the glass, and perched atop the brick sill was a little yellow bird. It had bright orange cheek patches and was no bigger than my palm. Its feathers were all fluffed and its beak rattled against the window with each fearful shake. The poor thing looked as if it had been flying around for a couple of days on an empty engine. First thing I did was to lock Mia out of the room so I could lure the timid creature inside with some almonds. The next thing I did was buy a cage and prayed I didn't unintentionally kill it.

My mission was to get him back home as soon as possible. I taped flyers around every neighborhood lamppost and placed ads all over the Internet—Craig's, Parrot911, and the local bird clubs. Three weeks went by and not one person responded. I was devastated. I had all but lost hope until I received an email from a woman named Ivana who claimed to be the owner. Finally, this little bird was about to be reunited with its flock again.

From: IvanaPolchowski <ivanapolchowski@gmail.com>
To: xtcbo-2908077664@comm.cl.org
Date: July 12, 2010, 6:23 a.m.

Subject: Found Bird

Hello Kelly,

My name is Ivana and I believe you have my bird. I respond to email only, so please give me your address and I will come and pick him up after 8 p.m. today

Many thanks,
Ivana

From: Kelly B <kellyb@hotmail.com>
To: IvanaPolchowski <ivanapolchowski@gmail.com>
Date: July 12, 2010 10:34 a.m.

Re: Found Bird

Hi Ivana,

Thank you so much for contacting me. Before I make arrangements to hand over the bird, could you please answer a few questions? What is the name that he responds to? Are there any unusual markings that would identify it as yours? And can you send over a picture of your missing bird so that I can make sure the bird I have is the same as yours?

Talk to you soon. Have a great day!
Kelly

From: IvanaPolchowski
To: Kelly B <kellyb@hotmail.com>
Date: July 12, 2010 1:46 p.m.

Re: Found Bird

Ms. Kelly,

I don't understand? Perhaps it is because my English is not so good. Why you ask so many questions? I told you bird is mine. It has been missing for couple weeks! Can you please give me your address and I will come today.

Thank you,
Ivana

From: Kelly B
To: IvanaPolchowski <ivanapolchowski@gmail.com>
Date: July 12, 2010 5:12 p.m.

Re: Found Bird

Hi Ivana,

Before I give away this little creature I want to make sure that
he is indeed yours. My questions come straight from a
licensed veterinarian. Answering them will put my mind at
ease. Afterwards, I will most certainly arrange for you to
come over to my house and pick the bird up. I'm sure he is
missing you.

Sorry for the inconvenience. I hope this clears things up a bit.

Thanks,
Kelly

From: IvanaPolchowski
To: Kelly B <kellyb@hotmail.com>
Date: July 12, 2010 7:46 p.m.

Re: Found Bird

I don't know who you are but think it very bad that you want
to question me like a criminal. I lost my bird, have I not
suffered enough? He was gift from my dead husband and I

miss him very much. I want him back. I come tonight. What your address????

***

A ten-alarm dilemma burned in my head. If Ivana really was the owner, why wouldn't she just answer at least one of my questions? Anyone that aggressive turned me into a skeptic. I decided to sleep on things and the next morning I placed a call to the Manhattan Bird Club for some advice. If anyone knew a thing or two about lost birds, surely it was them.

I spoke with a woman named Charlotte Steadman, the chapter president, who was kind enough to give me some guidance.

"We hear tons of stories like this all the time," she said. "Unfortunately, this is the problem with placing ads on the Internet. Any Tom, Dick or Jane can make wild claims and you never know what to believe. There are so many scammers out there looking for lost animals to make a quick buck—it's really despicable. The black market is full of illegal birds. Parrot breeding is big business."

"I can't believe an underground bird market is still going on in this day and age," I said.

"You better believe it! Most of the big parrots—Amazons, African Greys, you name it—are illegally smuggled in, ripped from their indigenous habitats and put up for sale here in the States. I don't want to point fingers, but you can believe the majority of birds you see for sale in the big name pet stores most likely got those animals through shady means. That is why the bird club keeps a database of names of known blacklist dealers. They're a sloppy bunch without a lot of imagination. Swap an I for and E here or there, but mainly it's all too easy to spot their names. I'll run this Ivana through our system and see if anything pops up."

"Thank you so much. I feel so bad for this little guy. It is so awful a person would want to take someone else's pet like that. It's crazy."

"You said your bird is an all yellow cockatiel, right?"

"Yes, I think so. Why? Is that bad?" I asked.

"No, no. Lutinos—that's the specific type of cockatiel you've got—are sold for at least a hundred and fifty dollars. These illegal breeders have warehouses set up like puppy mills. It's a sad life if a bird like yours is popular. They keep breeding them until the hens are egg-bound and die. That's why if you were to ever get a bird, check with us first, and we'll recommend reputable breeders."

"I don't know. I've got a cat. But then again, she shies away from the smallest things, especially kids and pocket-size Pomeranians. In fact it's the bird who is way more interested in her. This morning it tried using my cat's back as a helipad! The truth is, I heard birds are a lot of work and I'm not sure I'm up for the commitment. If this Ivana turns out to be some shady dealer, would you know of anyone who might take this bird? *He's really cute...*"

Charlotte laughed, "They're all cute, that's part of their charm! I suggest we look into Ivana before we make any alternative arrangements. Who knows, she might be who she says she is. It shouldn't take too long. Look out for an email later today."

Two hours later I received this response:

From: **Charlotte** <charlotte@manhattanbirdclub.com>
To: Kelly B <kellyb@hotmail.com>
Date: July 13, 2010 3:57 p.m.

Subject: Found Bird

Hello Kelly,

I'm afraid to report, the worst has come true. Ivana Polchowski's name popped up on our registry. You were very smart to go with your gut and contact us! According to what we know, she has been convicted more than three times for illegal bird trafficking. So I would definitely tell you to steer clear of her and contact the authorities. She's been using Craig's for a number of years to acquire lost animals. She has a particular interest in parrots like yours.

I spoke with a fellow member of the Manhattan Bird Club about the possibility of taking in your bird. Her name is Nancy Schillman and she is willing to meet with you. You can reach her at (212) 555-1000 to arrange a time to meet.

I always tell people looking to place homes for birds to ask lots of questions and check out the place before committing to anything. Good luck. If you have any more questions please don't hesitate to ask.

Charlotte

To: Charlotte <charlotte@manhattanbirdclub.com>
Date: July 13, 2010 4:32 p.m.

Re: Found Bird

Hi Charlotte,

Thank you so much for your help. I just spoke with the police and filed a report. Hopefully they will catch her before she moves on to another victim. I also wanted to let you know I contacted Nancy and we have plans to meet up this Saturday.

Once again, thanks for everything. It's so nice to know there are still some good people left out there!

Take care,
Kelly

***

Like the old spinster who lives in a studio apartment with fifty cats, or the alligator-sized rats that roam city sewers devouring young children, I always thought the crazy bird lady was rooted firmly in myth. But when Nancy attached a photo of herself along with a set of directions to her place, I was forced to reconsider my position on urban legends. The picture was one of those glamour shots taken in the depths of a suburban mall. Nancy sat in the middle, wide-eyed and grinning, while six small birds perched along each arm. A full crested cockatoo preened the top of her short gray hair, a golden retriever laid by her crossed feet, and, completing the jungle book shot, a black cat slept in her lap. Arched above them were the words, "Have a hoot of a holiday!" Below listed all sixteen of their names.

Who said animal lovers weren't crazy?

It was Saturday morning and I found myself at Nancy's door, listening to a cacophony of vivacious squawking and dog barking. The chorus started the minute I stepped out of the elevator, which was located halfway down the hall. I wondered what her next-door neighbors must have thought of her petting zoo. Judging from the noise, I was certain it couldn't be too good.

The door opened and Nancy greeted me with the same smile I recognized from the picture. Pacing behind her was an excited Golden Retriever, tongue dangling out the side of his mouth, nails clicking against the hardwood floor like an army of ballpoint pens.

"You must be Kelly—come on in," she grabbed hold of the dog's collar and shoved him aside. "I hope you don't mind all the noise. The animals love it when I get visitors. They think they're about to get treats."

I followed her down a long hallway lined with old black and white photographs and into an office-space which doubled as a bird sanctuary. On either side, cages filled the room with colorful chirping birds. Tucked in a corner was a writing desk stacked with thick piles of paper held down by glass weights. On the desk, perched on top of a reused wicker gift basket sat a gray cockatiel, staring solemnly out a tree-filled window.

"When I'm not grading college essays, I'm tending to these fellas. Over there are the latest to enter the family." She pointed to a cage with two small birds; their feathers were as bright as a pair of Granny Smith apples. One of them had a brace on its leg made from a broken toothpick. The way he hobbled across the wooden perch reminded me of Long John Silver. All he needed was a little sword and a captain's hat and he'd be a hit at Halloween parties.

"What's wrong with that one?" I asked.

"Oh, that's Buddy; he's got bumble foot. I made him that little brace because he can't walk so well anymore. He'll be like that forever, I'm afraid."

"Well at least he's in a good home," I reassured her. "How many animals are in here?"

"I play mommy to lots of little creatures. Currently I've got twelve birds, one dog, and a cat living here. I'm not sure how much Charlotte mentioned about me, but I am looking for a mate for my cockatiel, Lucky. He's been very depressed since he lost his partner."

She turned to the lone birdy by the window. I wandered over to say hi while Rufus, the resident dog, gave my leg a thorough sniff.

Lucky was speckled with grey and white spots and had a long crest that curled up at the end. His eyes were half closed. As I got closer, he pretended not to see me and looked the other way.

"Lucky seems sweet. What happened to his mate?"

There was long pause followed by a deep, regretful exhalation.

"You see, we are all vegetarian here, including the dog. Rufus just loves his tofu treats. Don't ya Rufus." She bent down and gave him a strategic pat on the head. "A few weeks ago, I had stepped out to pick up a couple of things at the supermarket. I must have forgotten to lock the cage door, and Lucky and his mate Tina escaped. It was the worst mistake I ever made. When I got back home, the apartment was oddly silent. I immediately knew something was wrong. That's when I rushed into this room and found Tina's feathers all over the floor and her little feet sticking out of Rufus's mouth. It was one of the most disturbing sights I have ever seen. There was nothing I could do to save her. Rufus ate her right in front of me."

Lucky puffed his feathers and gave a nervous shake. I shuddered in disbelief.

"Oh my god, that is so tragic! Poor Lucky and Tina! Your dog isn't still vegetarian, is he?" Surely after a gruesome episode like that, she'd switch the dog back to meat.

She looked at me like I had three heads. "Of course he's still a vegetarian. Why wouldn't he be?"

"I just figured with the accident and all, you might...you know what, never mind. It's none of my business." It was obvious Nancy didn't want to see a connection between a dog's need to eat meat and Tina the deceased. My eyes floated back to Lucky, sitting out in the open, a target practically painted on his back. No wonder the poor bird looked so depressed. He was living in fear of Rufus's next panic attack. "You aren't afraid Rufus will eat another bird?"

Nancy waved off the idea. "Oh no, he would never do that again. He told me himself."

"Really? How is that?"

"Rufus and I have a connection. A mommy knows these things. I can read it on his face. So this bird of yours, what kind of personality is he?"

"Super energetic, loud at times, and very inquisitive. When he wants to come out of his cage he does a really cute can-can dance."

"Is he fully flighted?"

"You mean are his wings clipped? No."

She frowned. "That might be a problem. You should know that I take a hands-off approach to birds."

"Meaning?"

"Well, I prefer keeping my birds wings clipped for safety and they usually remain in their cages the majority of the day. I hang out with all my animals but I'm not into giving them lots of affection, if you know what I mean."

"No, not really." I glanced at my phone and mentioned something about a text message. "This has been so nice," I said. "But I didn't realize the time. I have got to go."

"If you want I can lend you my carrier to bring your little guy here," Nancy offered.

"You know, that's OK. I've got something. Thanks anyway. I'll be in touch."

And with that, I left knowing I'd never step foot in her house again.

When I got home, I opened the cage and the little bird climbed out. He flew on my shoulder and let out a little tweet. Mia sauntered over, head-butted my shin and flopped over my feet. *Hands-off approach,* I thought. All I wanted to do was give these little fluffy creatures a good squeeze.

"So what do you say, Mia? Think we should keep him? It's a crazy world out there. You know, you've been there."

Mia curled her black and white striped tail around my leg, which I took as a yes.

"I'm going to have to name you, little birdy. I don't know if you're a boy or a girl. But you look like a Tony."

He leaned over and sealed the name with a kiss to my cheek.

Months later, after Tony laid her first egg I realized she wasn't the boisterous boy I originally thought. Nope, I landed myself a hen. The Romans used to say when a bird flies into your home and stays, it means a wind of change. From the moment Toni crawled through my window, I can assure you my life was never the same again.

posted: 2010-08-29 11:07 pm EDT

Studio Assistant Wanted (Greenpoint, Brooklyn)

I am looking for a part-time assistant to help me in my studio. Some of your job duties will involve constructing stretchers, preparing paints and prepping canvasses. You must be familiar with different power tools, including a circular and table saw. You must be able to follow directions and work independently. Attention to detail is mandatory.

Please send along your resume with a contact number so that I may call you to set-up an interview.

- Location: Greenpoint, Brooklyn
- It's NOT okay to solicit this person with services or other unrelated interests

From: Kelly B <kellyb@hotmail.com>
To: xtcbo-29080777664@comm.cl.org
Date: August 30, 2010 10:01 a.m.

Subject: Studio Assistant Position

To whom it may concern:

I am writing in reference to your Studio Assistant position. Currently, I am a freelance decorative painter/gold-leafer looking for part-time work. In addition to the decorative arts, I also do a lot of restoration work, which requires using tools and having plenty of patience when prepping delicate surfaces.

My most recent completed project was helping to build a small theater on 29th St. in Chelsea. I hand-painted over 15,000 ft of ceiling and column borders, upholstered walls, stained moldings, gold-leafed the ticket booth grill and hand-appliqued resin ornaments throughout the entire theater.

All of my previous jobs have required me to be meticulous, patient, and detail-oriented. I am a quick learner and follow instructions to a tee. Hopefully I have intrigued you enough to set up an interview. I would love the opportunity to further explain why I am a good fit for your studio assistant position.

I may be reached at (347) 512-1111 or by email. Attached is my resume for your review. Thank you so much for your time and consideration.

Take care,
Kelly

From: Dropsandots <dropsandots@gmail.com>
To: Kelly B <kellyb@hotmail.com>
Date: August 30, 2010 3:28 p.m.

Re: Studio Assistant Position

Hello Kelly,

I am contacting you about my studio assistant position. Will you be available to meet either Thursday or Friday this week? I am conducting interviews from 2:30 to 5:30 on these two days. Please let me know what day and hours work best for you. Have a good day.

Best,
Matteo

From: Kelly B
To: Dropsandots <dropsandots@gmail.com>
Date: August 30, 2010 8:53 p.m.

Re: Studio Assistant Position

Hi Matteo,

I'll take the Thursday at 4pm slot if it isn't filled yet. Any time after 3:30 p.m. works best for me. Thanks!

Take care,
Kelly

From: Dropsandots
To: Kelly B <kellyb@hotmail.com>
Date: August 31, 2010 8:14 a.m.

Re: Studio Assistant Position

Hi Kelly,

Thursday at 4pm it is. My address is 52-33 Ash St. The best way to get here is the G-train or by the #7. The studio doesn't have an intercom, so call me when you're downstairs and I will let you in. It's the big loft building on the corner. You can't miss it.

See you then.

Matteo

***

Matteo's loft was part of an old factory located on the fringe of city civilization, between the traffic-clogged artery of the Midtown Tunnel and rows of Polish pharmacies. This nugget of forgotten land on the northernmost tip of Brooklyn was my first introduction to Greenpoint. On the long walk from the subway station, I strolled amongst the low-slung industrial brick warehouses, remnants from a bygone maritime era and unbruised by vapid overdevelopment. These sleeping giants speckled the desolate waterfront block, and the only sound within an earshot was the faint hum of traffic floating across the East River. Behind a rusting chain-link fence, a clan of alley cats sprawled over the asphalt of an empty parking lot, soaking up the summer heat. Everywhere I looked the gilded cage of the New York City skyline opened itself upon me, whispering in my ear, begging me to see her in all her full, naked glory. A whole lifetime in New York, and never had I felt so alone and free. It was like coming home after fifty years to a city that changed its perfume—my senses were invigorated. I breathed it in, happy to know I had a few more minutes to spare before heading upstairs for my interview.

I decided to call my mom for a last-minute pep talk. I wanted her to say mom things like, *"You'll do great honey. This job has your name written all over it."* Instead, what I got was an earful about safety and not talking to strangers. How old was I, three? Next she was going to tell me to look both ways before crossing the street. It's amazing how parents can instantly pull you back into adolescence with a few well-chosen phrases, no matter what age.

"Mom, I know what I'm doing. You can stop worrying, OK? Don't believe everything you read in the papers. I'm positive Matteo isn't an axe murderer."

"I'm not trying to scare you, sweetheart. I just want you to be on guard, is all. There are all sorts out there. Look at what happened to those women last year..." Her voice quivered like it did every time she watched horrible events on the news, or moving Hallmark commercials. "Such a tragedy," she sighed. "I feel so bad for their parents."

"You act like I'm going on an interview with Jeffery Dahmer! Sheesh, not everyone is a serial killer, you know."

"Tell that to the parents whose children got murdered at the hands of that sicko."

"Mom...I called you for support. Instead of thinking about what to say on my interview, you've got my head swirling with refrigerated body parts. Thanks."

"OK, I'm sorry, you're right. You're an adult, I should trust you more. Knock 'em dead honey. Oops, should I not have said that now?"

"Look Mom, I gotta go. I'll call you when I'm done."

"Don't forget! I don't want to worry that you're lying in a ditch somewhere."

"*Goodbye, Mother!*"

I hung up and placed a called to Matteo, letting him know I was downstairs. A second later, a metal door covered in graffiti opened, and a man with thick, black curly hair and red rimmed glasses poked his head out. He reminded me of a young Antonio Banderas.

"Kelly?" he asked in a delectable Spanish accent.

"That's me." I stuck out my hand and he gave it a firm shake.

"Great. My studio is right upstairs. Don't let the hallway scare you. My landlord is allergic to cleaning."

"Don't worry, it takes a lot more than a dirty stairwell to scare me."

I followed him upstairs desperately trying to force my mother's paranoid thoughts out of my head. The inside of the building was a typical converted factory space: the brick hallways were half-painted and scribbled in places; concrete stairs were covered in a thick layer of dirt; sixteen foot ceilings towered above us, wearing nothing but their original floor braces. My mother's heart would explode of shock if she knew I was in such a place, and with a stranger, no less.

In comparison to the dark, cavernous labyrinth of hallways, Matteo's loft was bright, white, and airy. The midafternoon sun poured through a set of large windows and onto a row of cactus plants in terracotta pots. Occupying every inch of space, large and small paintings lay stacked against the walls in various forms of preparation.

Matteo fixed me a shot of espresso, and after a minute of banter he led me into his woodshop. Amidst the stacks of timber, colorful canning jars of paint, and bags of dried pigments, he pointed out the tools I needed to use.

"I paint on wood panels, so you'll need to cut a lot of wood and use the nail gun. You know how to use a circular saw, right?"

My hands went straight to my hips, akimbo style. "Sure, we had them laying all over the theater I worked in." I tried to sound like a real professional, despite the fact that I never actually used a circular saw, even if I was around plenty of them.

"Good. You know, I like that you are not an artist. Artists have too many opinions on how to do things. I need someone to follow instructions, not reinvent the wheel. Come let me show you some of my work, so you can see what I need you to do."

Matteo was a flurry of energy, so jacked up on espressos he was like a whirling dervish on steroids. A spin on his heel and we were back in the main room of his sunny studio, milling over several small paintings. Their surfaces glittered with tiny little droplets that looked like mesh fabric. The backgrounds were combinations of white, black, and vibrant reds.

"Some people say my work is obsessive," he said, running his fingers through his thick hair. "I never understood this."

"People who say stuff like that haven't done anything repetitive before. I spent months painting over fifteen hundred feet of intricate gold borders. Instead of finding it dreadful or boring, I actually enjoyed doing the same thing over and over again. It was all very Zen. I'm no art expert, but I can certainly see the calmness in your work."

The corner of his mouth curled up into a slight smile. "You know, you are one of the few who have ever got that at first glance. Maybe you should be writing my reviews."

"Well, I did go to school for writing. You never know what the future might hold." I laughed. "So how long are you looking to keep your assistant?"

"How long?" His dark inquisitive eyes sparkled. "I want an assistant for life, of course."

"Now that's what I'd call a permanent job. So when can we start?"

"Ah well, I have a few more interviews before I make any decision. In Spain, we say, '*Nunca es tarde, si la dicha es buena*'. It doesn't matter how long it takes, so long as the ending is good."

Once I learned he was from Spain, our conversation slowly steered away from job duties and Matteo's life as a painter, to how he came to New York, not knowing a soul, and why he had no plans to return home to his native country beyond the occasional holiday. We were having so much fun chitchatting, before we knew it an hour had passed and his next interview was downstairs.

"On to your next victim," I joked as I gathered my things to go. "Somehow, after this interview I don't think he'll be as fun and conversational as me."

"This was a job interview? I thought you were just dropping by for a cup of my coffee."

"Maybe I was! I guess only time will tell if you'll invite me back for another."

Matteo and I walked downstairs. Through the small glass window of the door I caught a glimpse at my competition. He was a shaggy-haired hipster, complete with a scruffy beard, skinny corduroys, and an ironic t-shirt. Poor thing, he didn't stand a chance after me.

Matteo leaned in and placed a friendly kiss on each cheek. It felt like a thousand tiny lightning bolts pricking my skin. In an instant I knew I'd be seeing him again.

"I should be done with all my interviews tomorrow. I'll let you know in a couple of days, when I reach a decision."

"However it turns out, it was a pleasure meeting you. Call me crazy, but I think we will meet again."

I waggled my fingers and left him with a parting smile. Matteo's next appointment waltzed by without a hint of a hello. *Good luck buddy,* I thought as the door slammed behind me. A second later my phone rang. It was my mother, right on cue.

"Hi there, honey," she said, trying to play it cool. "I was afraid you weren't going to pick up. How did the interview go?"

"You'll be happy to hear I'm still alive. I just got out now."

"*Now?* That was a long interview. What does the man paint? Murals like Donatello?"

"No, not quite. He was nice, from Spain. His paintings are beautiful and so is his place—fifteen hundred square feet! Can you believe he got here not knowing a soul, and his studio is the first and only place he's ever lived? Fifteen years in New York City and one apartment. Simply amazing. Talk about meant-to-be!"

"He lives there, too? You didn't tell me this before," she said as if I were holding out on some big secret.

"Oh, God Mom, not everything is some big conspiracy against you. It's one of these work-live lofts. Aren't you glad you didn't find out until now?"

"Maybe. So, you were up there for an hour. It went well, then?"

I touched the part of my cheek that still radiated from his kiss. "Let's say, I'd be very surprised if I didn't get the job."

"Of course you're going to get the job! How can anybody resist you?"

"Mom, I ask myself that question every day, and yet I still don't have a boyfriend."

"You will, honey. He's out there waiting. One day, you'll see. He'll come when you least expect it."

***

As I predicted, Matteo called me two days later with a job offer. The deal was this: work in his studio five days a week, for four hours a day, for the rest of eternity. I made him throw unlimited shots of espresso into the agreement, and I started work immediately.

For the first couple of weeks, I made peace with my fear of the circular saw and began sawing, hammering, nailing, cutting, and molding wood into stretchers, some reaching over seven feet high. Once I was fully covered in layers of sawdust and my fingers filled with splinters, Matteo switched my duties to paint-making. Like Michelangelo in his dark lair, I took scoops of colored pigments—Prussian blue, Mars black, Viridian green—and mixed them until they glimmered with saturation. Gradually with time and confidence, Matteo trusted me enough to let me try my hand at painting. I was a good student, and soon enough the two of us sat across the canvas, getting to know each other with instant intimacy. No subject was off limits: time travel, ancient civilizations, his failed marriage, my string of bad dates, why midday naps were good for the brain, and how—for better or worse—family means everything. Four months later, we were in winter and it felt like Matteo and I had known each other forever.

The holiday season had arrived and New York was in the mood to party. On every corner, Santas rang donation bells. Shoppers shuffled through slush and crowds to find that perfect gift for their special someone. Strings of Christmas lights twinkled like wet pearls, enveloping the city in a frosty white that turned the darkest drab days into a festive spectacular. Even this jaded city-slicker was caught up in the merriment. I unabashedly sipped too much eggnog, gorged myself at holiday parties, and over-decorated my Christmas tree with fervor. Kris Kringle had come early and wrapped me up in a blanket of Yuletide, and for the first time in many years, I felt truly happy. Then Matteo dropped a bomb: in a couple of days he was leaving me for Spain, and spending the holidays with his family.

"How long will you be gone?" I asked.

"One month. Any more and I'll lose my mind."

My heart sank. We spent so much time together; not seeing him every day was going to be an adjustment. I tried to mask my disappointment, but he must have sensed something.

"Don't worry," he said, placing a kind hand on my shoulder. "There is plenty of work left to do while I'm gone. We've got all those stretchers ready to be primed, remember?"

I swiped a hand across my head. "Whew, that's good news. I was nervous I wouldn't have enough work to buy you a special Christmas gift." I forced out a little laugh and kept my eyes on the painting.

"I should buy *you* the gift! After all, you have proven to be my best assistant ever."

The best assistant he's ever known. Just perfect. Perhaps some time apart would be good for me to gain some clarity. Too much time in the studio was clearly making me batty and causing me to misread feelings.

"So do you want me to bring something back from Spain?" he asked.

"How about a matador?"

"That might be a little hard. They are small, but I'm not sure I can squeeze one into my suitcase."

"OK, then just the bull will do," I said before burying my head back in my work.

It took three failed trips to JFK at the height of holiday rush-hour traffic before Matteo finally said *adios* to New York, and *hola* to his native land. While he was at home nibbling on tapas and sipping tempranillos, I was hunkered down in the studio, blasting my way through his complete Pixies collection, priming canvases. Day in and day out, I strapped on my paint-stained apron and worked until my arms ached. It wasn't the same, being alone. I longed for Matteo's conversation. I was bored and needed distraction. One day while on my lunch break, I set out on an exploration of the studio, starting with a peek inside the medicine cabinet. Besides aspirin and a year's supply of dental floss, there were no exciting discoveries to be made in the bathroom. I didn't know what I was searching for, but my curiosity led me upstairs to a spare room I had never seen before.

The room was small and spartan. There was a bookcase filled with catalogues chronicling Matteo's career and a stash of old paintings. It was hardly mysterious, yet the space had an inexplicable affection that took hold of me. I grabbed a catalogue, plopped down on the floor in the sunniest spot of the room, and began reading. Halfway through an essay comparing Matteo's work to Jackson Pollock's, a small photograph fell into my lap. It was Matteo—his hair was several inches longer and parted in a mass of little black ringlets. He had on a black motorcycle jacket, funky sunglasses, and wore a goofy smile, as if someone had just told him a dirty joke. Scribbled on the back was the place and date: L.A., 1998. The thunderbolt pricked me again. This time I knew what it meant.

***

It's funny how if you're open enough to the signs, life can quite literally paint your way. The day before Christmas Eve, planted in my mailbox like a little prophecy, was a holiday card from my mom. It wasn't the usual sort—reindeer or jingle bells, happy Santas, or candy canes. The image on the front was a fifteenth-century etching of a knight in armor. Inside, all she wrote was: *Hope your knight comes and whisks you away. Happy Holidays.*

Did she know something I didn't? Maybe I'd yammered on for too long about a certain someone and blown my subconscious wide open? Whatever it was, the card was a strange reminder—where the hell was that damn knight of mine? Eating croquettas and basking under Spain's famous sun, I was sure. I placed the card on my bed stand like a vigil and lit a candle every night. I thought if I stared at the knight long enough, he would appear.

Two weeks later he did, bearing a gift in his hand.

"A little something from Spain," Matteo said, passing me a small wrapped package. "It's not much, but I think you'll like it."

"Not a matador?" I joked.

"No," he said with a frown. "I tried, but they caught him at customs. He's on a plane back to Spain as we speak."

I felt his eyes watching me as I opened it up. Inside was a small wooden fan carved with an intricate Moorish design.

"Matteo, it's beautiful. Gracias!" I gave him a peck on the cheek and passed him a tin box from my purse.

"What is this?" he asked.

"Just a little something for you."

"Kelly, you shouldn't have."

I put a finger to my lips. "Nonsense. I went a little crazy with my baking. I hope you like chocolate chip cookies. They go best with a nice cup of coffee."

"I think I have just the thing."

Matteo pulled out a can of freshly ground Italian roast and whipped us up a couple of frothy cappuccinos. In between sips and nibbles, we caught up on things. Afterwards, we took our spots at opposite ends of a bright red canvas and spent the next few hours painting. By eight o'clock my eyes were aching and I knew it was time to leave. I stood up and rested my tired sight on the window. Outside, there was nothing to see but a sheet of white. Snowflakes as large as fists floated down in thick swirling bands. At least four inches of snow had fallen in the time we were painting.

"I didn't realize how bad it is out there," I said. "The news said some flurries, not a blizzard. Looks like the weatherman got it wrong, *again*. What is their accuracy rate—something like forty-nine percent? It's coming down really hard, I hope I don't get snowed in."

Matteo joined me at the window. "We can check the news if you want. If it's really bad, you can always stay here."

"That's nice of you, but let's see what the news says first. I've got animals that need feeding."

He flicked on the television and we both hovered close together as a red band scrolled across the bottom of the screen. Blizzard warning in effect for all five boroughs until 3

222

a.m. Mayor warns residents to stay home and off the streets. Whiteout conditions expected. Wind gusts up to 40mph.

We looked at each other.

"So what would you like to do?" he asked.

I walked back to the window. A sheet of hail and snow danced across the screen.

"I don't know." I wanted to stay, but was afraid of what might happen if I did. My last slumber party with a man ended in disaster. If something went wrong, I wouldn't be able to call a cab and escape. If I stayed, it was a commitment.

"Like I said, you can always spend the night here if you like...that is if you don't mind sharing a bed. I'd sleep on a sofa if I owned one. Or I can ask around, see if any of my neighbors have an airbed."

"No, no, that's ok. No need to go through the trouble."

"If you are worried—you have permission to kick me if I snore too loud."

"I trust you won't take advantage of my vulnerable situation?"

He placed a palm over his heart. "Of course not, you have my word."

I deliberated for a moment. "Ok then. I guess I should call my neighbors and get my pets sorted out."

"You do that, and I'll prepare us a nice dinner."

My stomach fluttered as if I had swallowed a moth.

***

That night, Matteo kept his promise. He stayed on his side of the bed, didn't hog all the blankets, and even refrained from

223

snoring in my ear. Under the covers we played it safe; the invisible line was as solid as the Mason-Dixon. Not a toe budged over the divide while we both struggled to fall asleep. But under the heaviness of slumber, none of our carefully plotted boundaries lasted. The next morning I awoke entwined in the warm comfort of Matteo's arms. For the first time in ages, I could not remember a single dream. Somehow the fantasy was replaced with a real sense of security. It felt so right and so natural; part of me wished we could lie there together forever.

He must have sensed I was awake because beneath the sheets his feet began to stir. I turned and faced him. His eyes were barely open, still filled with sleep. I didn't think about anything, instinct took over. I closed my eyes, leaned in and kissed him. His face remained still. Regret churned around my head. *Bad move Kelly, bad move!* I was ready to leap out of bed and pretend nothing happened when a slow smile crept across his face.

"Am I dreaming?" he asked.

"No, I don't think so," I whispered.

"Good."

"Good? You sure?"

He nodded his head. "Si."

"What do we do now?" I asked.

"Kiss again."

"But then everything changes."

"Yes, only for the better."

He leaned in and kissed me as if it was the first time all over again.

posted: 2011-06, 15 10:51 am EDT

***Excellent Pet House Sitter Avail 4 You! ***

*Seeking solitude in environment w/positive energy conducive for creative endeavors. Yr apartment must be smoke-free, have computer, in a safe setting near the water or close walk to town. Minimum of 1 wk, but seek longer times to write. *Will only respond to Serious Inquiries. Exclusively Excellent References procured if needed.

*Enjoy peace of mind. Travel w/confidence and return to happy healthy pets. Yr beautiful home is secure + added benefit yr saving significant $$$. The sanctity of yr space is guaranteed. You appreciate the value of such a special opportunity.

*Me: Professional, highly educated, kind, integrity-driven scribe/educator, Columbia University Alumni. Neat & well versed in home maintenance. Have green thumb, will take care of yr treasured home, pets, flora, as if they were my own.

*Interested? Respond to link above. State availability + share all: pets involved/special needs/photos/travel dates/location/brief description of yr living env't/contact info *Thank You + yr best friend(s) will also Thank You!

- Location: New York, NY
- It's NOT okay to solicit this person with services or other unrelated interests

Barter

From: Kelly B <kellyb@hotmail.com>
To: 7nhvrt-1408569543@sale.cl.org
Date: June 17, 2011 11:38 a.m.

Subject: Excellent Pet/House Sitter Avail 4 You!

Hello,
My name is Kelly and I am responding to your ad for a pet
sitter/house sitter. I have just begun my search to find the
perfect person to slip into my home for 3 weeks and take care
of a sweet cat and small charismatic bird (cockatiel) while I
visit my boyfriend's family in Spain this July.

We live in a sunny large work/live loft in Greenpoint
Brooklyn, on a quiet waterfront street. Nearby is a great
organic supermarket and an charming video store run by a
former manager of the Film Forum. If you love to cook, we
have a fully equipped kitchen at your disposal. A washing
machine is on the premises. 7 minute walk to train station.

Our main goal is to find someone loving, knowledgeable of
animals (especially comfortable w/birds), responsible and
clean. My boyfriend and I work from home and our pets are
used to a certain amount of company. We've had artist
friends come for shorter stays. They treat our place like an
artist retreat, and in exchange, they keep our little ones

227

company while we travel. Ideally, we are seeking a similar arrangement. If this interests you, I can be reached at this email address or by telephone (718) 555-5240. Look forward to hearing from you.

Take care,
Kelly

From:**Pawsandclaws**<pawsandclaws@gmail.com>
To: Kelly B <kellyb@hotmail.com>
Date: June 20, 2011 5:19 a.m.

Re: Excellent Pet/House Sitter Avail 4 You!

Hello Kelly,

Yr place sounds magical and yr pets adorable. I am a writer and work w/Columbia University so I need access to a computer. Does yr apt have one? This is a deal breaker. I love being by water, grew up in the Cape of Massachusetts w/2 dogs, 5 cats and couple of parakeets. Yr place sounds perfect for creative solitude. Pls send me yr dates of travel and we can discuss over phone my list of services. Phone # is (917) 873-1920.

Warmly yours,
Carolyn

From: Kelly B
To: Pawsandclaws <Pawsandclaws@gmail.com>
Date: June 20, 2011 2:36 p.m.

Re: Excellent Pet/House Sitter Avail 4 You!

Sounds great, Carolyn. I will give you a call tonight, say 6ish? Drop me a line if this time is no good. Otherwise, I can't wait to chat later. Thanks!
Ttly,
Kelly

When I didn't hear back from Carolyn, I picked up the phone and called her at six p.m. on the dot. The phone barely ran once when an out of breath woman answered. "Hello? Kelly? Is that you?" Judging from the sound of her voice, I pegged her for someone in her late sixties.

"Hi Carolyn, this is Kelly. I'm calling about the pet sitting."

"Yes, yes."

"So nice to place a voice to your email. I've never done this kind of thing before, so I'm not sure how this goes. As I mentioned earlier, my boyfriend and I are going to Spain for the month of July—"

"Oh that's a lovely country. Just lovely." A tea kettle howled in the background. "I was in Spain ages ago. Lost my passport, fell in love with a gypsy and the rest is history."

"That's adventurous! Care to elaborate?" I asked.

"No. That chapter closed many years ago."

Awkward pause.

"Ah, okay," I said into the silence. "Maybe you want to tell me a little bit about yourself? You said you work for Columbia. What kind of work do you do?"

"Oh, a little bit of this and that. Mainly, I teach English to business travelers."

"And you do this through the University?"

"No, no. Strictly private clients."

"Oh, okay. You mentioned you were a writer?"

"Yes." Her answer was quick and swift.

"And you write for Columbia? Do I have that straight?"

"Sometimes I write, yes. This is why I need a computer. You do have a computer, yes? I said that was a deal breaker. I also require internet access."

I reassured her that we had both. She seemed relieved by this. I, on the other hand, grew more suspicious. What was with the computer business? I thought Columbia had thousands of them on campus.

"Oh, I just love all sorts of critters," Carolyn continued. "I've watched and owned many animals. Many, many, animals. I even took care of a horn-nose lizard once. Oh, Boris—he had the worst breath ever. He always wanted to lick me when I watered the plants. The vet said he had advance gum disease. He wound up getting half his teeth pulled at that visit. Did I mention I have quite the green thumb? Quite the green thumb, indeed. If you have special plant needs, I will need to know that information beforehand. But I don't do orchids—they *do not* like me. So if you have a lot of orchids in your place, I make no promises."

"No worries, no orchids. So what is your availability for the month of July?"

"July is wide open. Wide, wide, wide. You know, July always reminds me of that old song—'Yankee Doodle Dandy.' You do know the one I speak of, yes? What a wonderful song, that one is. As I was saying, I think we should meet in person before moving forward. I'm sure us humans and your darling pets would do for a proper introduction, no? Do you know the dates of travel yet?"

"Travel dates?" My mind was still stuck on "Yankee Doodle Dandy" and Boris the horn toad lizard's gum disease. "No, we haven't bought our tickets yet. But I will keep you posted. So how is next week for an in-person meet?"

"I only do Fridays. Friday is a good karma day."

"Well, we want good karma, so then Friday it is."

Over the course of the week, emails bounced between us and ultimately we chose to meet at a little café around the corner from my apartment called Milk and Roses. It had all the old-world Brooklyn charm everyone loved nowadays—tin ceilings, old cracked leather sofas, round tables, and a chatty Italian owner who harked all the way from Bologna. It was quaint and casual, and had a laidback vibe perfect for a first time meeting. If the interview was a bust, at least we had some decent coffee.

Matteo and I arrived at the café a few minutes before noon Friday morning. Carolyn had been very explicit about our meeting time, and the last thing I wanted to do was be late. While I grabbed a vacant table next to the window, Matteo said hello to the owner and ordered a round of espressos at the counter. A moment later, two warm cups were settled in front of us. Their sweet, nutty fragrance perfumed the air. I checked the time on my phone, it was five past twelve: Not a sign of Carolyn anywhere.

Forty-five minutes later, Matteo stood up and tossed a couple of bills on the table.

"That's it. I'm done waiting for some crazy lady. Come on, let's get out of here."

My eyes remained fixed on the window; I didn't want to believe we had been stood up. How could she, especially when she had made such a fuss over the specifics? "I don't understand. Should I call her? Maybe something happened."

"She's not coming Kelly, come on, *nos vamos.*" Matteo grabbed my hand and pulled me to my feet. "Maybe she wrote you an email."

"Email? Why in the world would she do that when she's got my cellphone number?"

"You told me yourself she was a bit of a loony. Anything is possible."

"I guess. I was holding out because so far she's our only prospect. I had to give her some consideration."

"Well, consider her a no-go. Time to head home. I'm done wasting time here."

Back at the ranch, the first thing I did was turn on my computer and check my inbox.

"Matteo, you were right. She sent us a message..."

Sitting there like a gleaming piece of bad news, was Carolyn's email sent twelve minutes after our appointed meeting time. I couldn't believe it—while Matteo and I were waiting for her, she was busy typing out her excuse.

From: Pawsandclaws
To: Kelly B <kellyb@hotmail.com>
Date: July 1, 2011 12:12 p.m.

Re: Brooklyn Meet-up

Dearest Kelly,

My sincerest apologies but I won't be able to make it to Brooklyn this morning. My dear friend and her dog tragically died in a fire early today. Both funerals are this morning and I need to go and say my goodbyes. For obvious reasons, the conflict of schedules has forced me to cancel our meeting. Yr such a good person I know you will be understanding of this devastating news I bring.

Yr blessings are most welcome in this time of distress. I will make a prayer for you at the funeral.

Warmest regards,
Carolyn

Dead dog *and* dead friend? Was she kidding me? Her excuse reeked from a mile away. I was fuming. My eyes narrowed into slits as I sat there wondering how I should deal with the situation. Read her the riot act? Or adopt a Buddhist philosophy and let it go? So much deliberating; high road, low road. *Oh forget it.* I slapped shut my laptop and walked away.

Matteo saw my red-splotched face and gave me a consoling hug. "You should try to let it go, honey." His wet voice soothed into my ear. "We probably dodged a bullet with that one. If you ask me, she sounded crazy."

I broke away. "I'm *waaay* too pissed to let it go. You should read all the emails she sent—insisting I showed up on time, and look at what she does! She has the audacity to write some lame excuse twelve minutes *after* she's supposed to meet us? I don't know what you would call it in Spain, but I call it downright fucking rude! 'Dead friend' my ass; I don't believe her for a second."

Matteo wandered over to the kitchen and grabbed two cookies from a tin. The tactic was to sweeten me up so I would drop the matter. I took the cookie, but I didn't take the bait.

"What do you make of all this?" I asked. "You think she was telling the truth?"

"No. No way."

"Am I a cruel person to think she's a liar?"

"You? Cruel? Not a chance." He brushed a couple of crumbs off the corner of my mouth. "She's the cruel one for wasting our whole morning. She stood us up and then lied to cover her tracks. Dead dog and friend, both with funerals today?" He shook his head. "I've never heard of such a thing."

"Maybe you're right."

"Of course, I'm right," he laughed. "I'm always right. Now what you should do is send her a letter."

"But you just said a minute ago—"

"Forget about what I said earlier. I know you're never going to get over this if you don't say something."

"But what if she starts writing me a whole bunch of crazy nonsense? I don't know if I want to deal."

He looked at me deadpan. "What do you care what she says? We are not going to hire her. Do it, and you'll see how much better you feel afterwards."

"Fine," I huffed. "I'll write something once I've cooled down. I'm too pissed off to think."

"Don't wait too long," he insisted. "Right now anger is your weapon."

By dinnertime, I couldn't stand it any longer. Time hadn't cooled me down; in fact it acted like an accelerant to the roaring kiln in my belly. I knew if I didn't write a response soon, I was going to explode all over my keyboard, like a festering case of liquid diarrhea. It was time to grab that bottle of Pepto and get writing. I stared at the blinking cursor on the empty page and I chanted in my head: *I am a Zen master, I am a Zen master, I am a Zen master...*When that didn't work, I got all Terminator on her ass. It was so much more satisfying.

From: Kelly B
To: Pawsandclaws <Pawsandclaws@gmail.com>
Date: July 1, 2011 9:26 p.m.

Re: Brooklyn Meet-up

Dear Carolyn,
You have some nerve. What kind of person sends an email 12 minutes AFTER you are supposed to be somewhere? My boyfriend and I waited over 45 minutes for you. You had my cell phone number, you easily could have called. Instead you

send me an email?! Who does that? Apparently, cowards like you.

Not only is your behavior rude, it is simply unacceptable. How could I ever trust my home and animals in your care if you can't even be bothered to show up at an appointed time? Especially when you knew there were two people waiting for you!!! If this is how you treat people, it is no wonder your friends die on you.

I do not believe a word you said and I think you are a big fat liar. We won't be needing your services. Good luck with finding another sucker.

You can take your warmest regards and shove it up your ass, Kelly

---

From: Pawsandclaws
To: Kelly B <kellyb@hotmail.com>
Date: July 2, 2011 12:54 a.m.

Re: Brooklyn Meet-up

Why I never!! How dare you make such accusations against my character. I should sue you for slander!

My friend and her dear Cockapoo, Euclid, died tragically in a fire and you shamelessly mock it?! What kind of person are you to make fun of a person's unfortunate demise? She SPONTANIOUSLY COMBUSTED and accidently SET

HER DOG on FIRE!!! Why on earth would I make something like that up? Perhaps you want proof? Euclid's burnt jawbone maybe?

Yr a sick, sick, sick individual and you need to have yr head examined. You should know I have reported you to the authorities on Craig's. I told them all about the situation and yr harassing email. I hope they ban you for life! My only wish is that I may spare another person from such a terrifying experience.

Go rot in hell like the rest of the devils.
May God bless your wretched soul.

Well now. If I could reach through the computer screen and toss her a big fat punch, this woman would be seeing the aurora borealis by now. I had fantasies of slamming her head so hard it would rattle like a cowbell for days. She wanted to declare war and report me to Craig? She was nothing but a keyboard gangster. I called her bluff and threw up this fake ad to see if I got flagged. It was nothing short of a catastrophe.

posted: 2011-07, 02 12:27 pm EDT

Free Bedbug Mattress Giveaway (Greenpoint)

Ah yeah, you heard that right. It's me baby, that sprawling California King you've always dreamed of having but couldn't afford. Well now you can own a piece of luxury. Best part—I'm free! All I need is the right person to whisk me away. Come and pick me up, and I promise I'll get you laid. You're not scared of a couple of bedbugs, right? I promise I won't bite too much.

For all you takers, I'll be waiting on the corner of Franklin and India wrapped up in my finest plastic. If no one comes to claim me by 5 pm, no worries, I'll just crawl away on my own.

- Location: Greenpoint, NY
- It's NOT okay to solicit this person with services or other unrelated interests

The ad was only up for a matter of minutes when I received an email from one of Craig's moderators. Shit, this was not looking good.

From: HelpMeCraig <helpmecraig@cl.org>
To: Kelly B <kellyb@hotmail.com>
Date: Saturday, July 2, 2011 12:42 p.m.

Subject: You've been flagged

Dear Ms. Brixi,
This is a notice from the HelpMeCraig office, the anti-harassment unit at Craig's.org. This is a letter informing you that your account with us has been flagged.

Our office received a recorded account of harassment from poster, Carolyn Hynes at Pawsandclaws@gmail.com. This is a very serious accusation and we at HelpMeCraig take harassment matters with the utmost importance. As a result, Craig's.org has blocked your activity pending further notice. Our office will be reviewing these allegations in accordance with Section1546-#2BA of our Terms of Agreement. This means you will no longer be able to reply to or place any posts until the situation is resolved.

You have ten business days to state your case, upon which there will be a review of all the supported documents. A determined outcome will be established from the HelpMeCraig staff. If our office finds you innocent of the allegations, HelpMeCraig will lift the block levied against you. If you are to be found guilty of harassment, you may face further penalties and your case will be passed onto our legal department. You will receive confirmation from the HelpMeCraig office within a month of our decision.

If you do not respond within ten business days, Craig's.org will consider the allegation of harassment to be true, and you will be permanently banned from all future Craig's.org activity.
We strive to keep Craig's.org a safe and secure place. Thank you for your patience and understanding.

Sincerely,
James Madison
Sr. VP. Operating Officer of Harrassment
HelpMeCraig Staff

Fuck. Fuck. Fuck!

I read the correspondences that Carolyn forwarded to the HelpMeCraig staff and it was full of deleted lines and inserted fallacies. A few well poised swipes of her fingers, and she had effectively turned me into a heartless bitch—someone who made fun of funerals and dead animals. She had gone too far and now she needed to pay.

I didn't bother writing back to the HelpMeCraig people. I went straight to the top of the food chain. If anyone was going to nail this woman to the cross, it would be my old friend.

Dear Craig,

Boy oh boy, has it been a while! I miss you! Every day I hear someone talking about you and your company. It must be so strange to be a household name. God, it's hard to imagine it's been eleven years since you arrived in NYC. You didn't know a soul, and now look at you—a full-fledged celebrity! You conquered New York and are still here. Not many people have guts to stick it out like you. Most transplants move back to their parents' basements because they can't hack the pressure—or worse, buy a house out in the suburbs when they start having babies. Oh, how they come and go like flies on a spider web, ravaged by time and sadistic temptations. But you, my dear friend, you are still around even after the bad press and the devastating tragedies. As a New York City ambassador, it's high time I started calling you a native. You've gotta have brass balls and an elephant's skin to survive in this town. Welcome to the club, you're officially an insider!

There are so many BIG things to fill you in on, but before I can get to the good stuff, I have a delicate matter I must discuss with you first. Recently I met someone (yes, I swear I'll get to him in a minute) and things are looking good. I moved into his place in Brooklyn a few months ago, and now I'm about to meet his family for the first time. Talk about nerve-wracking! Oh—did I mention they all live in Spain and don't speak a lick of English? Anyhoo, I found a woman off your site who advertised herself as a house-sitter.

After failing to arrive at our appointed time, she had the nerve to give a lurid excuse of having to go to the unexpected funeral of a friend and her dog who died from a rare case of spontaneous combustion. When I called her on her bullshit, she reported me to your helpdesk, where it seems I am currently on trial for harassment.

This is the biggest crock of shit I've heard since the word Ebonics was introduced into the English vernacular. Since we go way back, could you do the honors and set the record straight? I wouldn't know what to do if I was banned from your site. Where else am I going to find that ergonomically correct desk chair for such a good price, or find out about the next backgammon meet-up? Don't you see: I'd be lost without your lists! Please, Craig, you have to help me!

But before I repulse you with such blatant begging, I'd like to talk about love and how I'm swimming in it. As you can tell, life has gotten soooo much better since I last wrote. Sure, I had to gain and lose twenty pounds, ban all forms of dairy, get a new job, and adopt a couple of pets before it arrived. But now that the love is here to stay, I reason all my godawful dates must have been the universe's way of not spoiling me too quickly. One of the best parts of being in love is that I have you to thank for it. If it weren't for that random job listing, I might have never met Matteo. I promise, if we get married—I know it's premature, but we're talking about doing a little ceremony in Rome—we want you to be our officiant. I can't think of anyone more suited for the task then the one who brought us together.

Ever wonder how many other people you have inadvertently married? I bet it's a bunch. When people ask how we met, I love saying we met through your site. You should see how their eyes light up! Who knew finding love online could be so cool, and it's all because of you...

Forever yours,

Kelly

From: HelpMeCraig@cl.org <helpmecraig@cl.org>
To: Kelly B <kellyb@hotmail.com>
Date: Sunday, July 3, 2011 7:19 a.m.

Re: You've been Flagged

Dear Ms. Brixi,

Congratulations! We at the HelpMeCraig office would like to officially inform you, after careful consideration of the facts, the temporary ban on your account has been lifted, effective immediately.

We looked into Ms. Hynes harassment complaints and found them to be unsubstantiated. Subsequently, upon further inspection we have deemed her false allegations were in direct violation with our Terms of Agreement. As a result, Ms. Hynes may no longer be allowed on Craig's site. If you see any related material in which you believe to be from her, please contact us immediately. Someone from the

HelpMeCraig staff will be on hand to swiftly remove any of her posts from our system.

Please accept our apologies over this unfortunate experience. We encourage you to take full advantage of our site's offerings—whether it be that secondhand office chair you've been eyeing, or an upcoming backgammon event in your neighborhood.

Okay, now that we've got the formalities out of the way...

Wow, a wedding in Rome? Of course, I will be your officiant. Nothing would make me happier. After all these years, I never thought I'd see the day you turned into such a romantic. You know, you are not the only one with beans to spill. There is someone I want you to meet. Her name is Laura and she is the most beautiful creature on earth. I spend my life online and yet we met the old fashion way, by bumping into each other on the street. Life moves in the strangest way; you really never know what type of curve ball might land in your mitt.

How about we make plans for dinner and catch up? There's this new restaurant that just opened by my place a month ago. We'd better make reservations now before the place blows up. Leave it to me, I'll pull out my cool card and get us a primo spot. Call it an occupational hazard, but it's good to be on a list every now and then.

Forever your dear friend,
Craig

ACKNOWLEDGEMENTS

I am eternally grateful to everyone who had a hand in making this book possible. For the love of my life, Teo, this book wouldn't exist without you. A gazillion thanks to my family and friends for putting up with my endless yammering—I promise it won't happen again until I come out with my next novel. A mountain of thanks to my fabulous team who added that extra shine in all the right places: Tracey Berglund for her brilliant cover ideas and Robert Rodi for his insightful edits.

And lastly, a very warm thanks to Craig Newmark. Without his site, I would never have met my husband or one of my best friends, landed myself a life-changing gig, or had so much fun in the wacky world of online advertisements.

KIM MASSON is a writer, reporter, and native New Yorker. When she is not covering the Brooklyn news beat, she's concocting stories that jab at the heart and tickle the feet. You can connect with her at www.kimmassonwrites.com or on social media @kimasson.